THE CRYSTAL SCREW

Monitor lizard, Horace Avraham, has always steered his best friend and boss in the right direction. Only this time, Lenox is ignoring his advice.

Victor Lenox is a cheerfully corrupt ward-heeler who aspires to something better: the daughter of Senator Jared Wilson Vale, the heiress to a dynasty of political purebred dalmatians. Does he want her badly enough to commit murder? And if Lenox is innocent, which of his dozens of enemies is doing an awfully good job of framing him?

Can Avraham solve the puzzle in time, or will the next stop be the gas chamber?

.

The Crystal Screw

A Poached Parody

P.C. HATTER

Also known as Stacy Bender

Byrnas Books

The Crystal Screw

Cover Design by Elizabeth Mackey
Art by Sara "Caribou" Miles

ISBN: 9798553941161

CHAPTER 1

The dice rolled across the table, bounced off the rim, and came up six and two. While the winners cleared the table of money, I hissed at another loss. A weasel picked up the dice, said, "Shoot two-bits," and dropped a twenty and a five on the table.

I stepped back. "I'm going to refuel." The walk across the billiard room would have normally been uneventful. Most people tended to leave monitor lizards alone, but the desperate hamster grabbed my arm.

"D-d-did you t-talk to V-v-victor?" The hamster looked up at me pleadingly, his stutter more pronounced with worry.

"I'm heading in that direction now, Richey. But these things take time, so don't expect much."

"B-b-but she's having a b-b-baby next month."

This was news to me, and I automatically placed this new information into the equation I'd been working on, and it altered the results. But not in a good way. The first thing I did was brush the hamsters hand off my arm. "It's a bad time, Richey. Don't expect much until November." Before the hamster could get out his first word, I said, "I'll tell him the situation, but you know that dog is in a tough spot right now, and he's limited on what he can do."

Richey blinked several times before saying, "G-g-go up now. I-I'll wait."

I walked up the stairs to the second-floor landing, tasting the air, and lit a cigar before knocking on an oaken door.

"Come in." At the dog's words, I entered to find Victor Lenox standing at the window with his hands in his

1

pockets, staring at the street below. When I'd first met the pit bull, I'd thought he was one of the purebreeds, but somewhere in his ancestry another breed or breeds entered the line changing the contours of his face. He turned and smiled at me. "I was wondering when you'd show up."

"Could you lend me two-hundred? There's a race, and I'd like to put money on Shadow Dancer."

"It's been a while since you've won anything." Victor pulled out his wallet, extracted the cash, and handed it over. "Isn't Excalibur your favorite runner?"

"First, Shadow Dancer runs better on a wet track, and it's supposed to rain. Second, Excalibur's love life's been leaked to the newspapers. Bit of a scandal involving a Clydesdale, so that horse isn't going to have his mind on getting to the finish line. If he gets to the track at all. Mind if I use your phone?"

Lenox motioned to the telephone sitting on the desk, and I picked up the receiver, dialed, and waited as the other end rang.

"Hello?" came a voice when someone finally picked up.

"Daniel, this is Horace Avraham. What's the price for Shadow Dancer?" The squirrel rattled off the stakes, and I did a quick calculation before placing my bet and hanging up.

"You could take a break when you hit these sour patches, you know."

"That would only lengthen the streak. No, if I can stand, I'll stand."

"Mom wants an explanation as to why you haven't been around to the house. You'd better soon before she comes looking for you, and you know how she is."

With a nod, I said, "I'll stop by sometime this week, for dinner maybe."

The air in the room tasted off, and I realized something was worrying the dog. "Is that what you called me in here for?"

"Yes... no... well, I need some advice." Lenox

coughed, took a deep breath, and held his hands behind his back. "Wendy Vale's birthday is Thursday, and I was wondering what to get her."

My first thought was that he was joking, but from the look on his face, I knew he wasn't. "Are they having some sort of party?" When he nodded, I asked, "Are you invited?"

"No, but I'm having dinner with them tomorrow."

I looked down at my cigar, organizing my thoughts. "Are you going to back Senator Vale?"

"I should think so."

"And your reason for doing so?"

"With us behind him, the dalmatian can win, and with him on our side, we can clean up the election."

Nodding, I asked, "Can he win without you this time?"

"No, and he knows it." Lenox's eyes narrowed. "What are you getting at?"

"Not getting at anything, but don't you think the rest of the ticket needs support?"

"Tickets can never get enough support, but if you're asking if we can hold our own without him, I'd say yes. But if you're asking if I've made any promises, let's just say that we've come to an understanding."

Lenox was being cagey, and as much as I wanted to understand why, the whole situation stank and not in a good way. "Drop him in a hole and bury him."

The dog growled, showed his teeth, and slammed a fist onto the desk. "What is it with you? Everything goes along just fine, then you decide to throw a wrench into the works."

The short burst of anger dissipated as Lenox cocked his head to the side and wagged his thin tail.

"Okay," I said. "Answer me this. Will the dalmatian play ball with you after he gets re-elected?"

Lenox barked a laugh. "Don't worry about him. I'll handled the Senator."

"And just how far has that daughter of his messed up

your head?"

"I'm going to marry Wendy Vale."

With a hiss, I crushed my cigar out in a brass ashtray on the desk. "Is that part of the deal?" When Lenox didn't answer right away, I added, "I won't say anything, but you'd better get that agreement in writing, notarized, and marry the female before the election. Then you'll have your pound of flesh."

The pit bull looked away, and his ears flattened as his tail stopped moving. "The Senator is an honorable male. I do wish you'd stop talking about him like he was a street mongrel."

"He's a purebred aristocrat. One of the few left in politics. That's why I'm telling you to be wary and watch your back. That dog plays by his own rules, and you're not in his class. His rules don't apply to mutts."

Lenox let out a whine, but before he could speak, I added, "And what about that pup of his? Ben Vale is also an aristocrat, and you broke up his dalliance with your daughter. How's that going to work out? I realize canines aren't as strict about breeding lines as horses, but would the Senator tolerate all mutts for grandpuppies?"

The pit bull let out a growl. "I just asked you what I should get Wendy as a present."

Pushing Lenox too far wasn't a good idea. While the dog was good natured, he had a temper and a jaw that could lock if the situation called for it. "How far have you gotten in your courtship?"

"There hasn't been any. I've only met her at the Senator's place and not every time. I know her well enough to say hello and haven't had a chance to talk to her."

"And you're already planning a wedding? I never realized you were such a romantic." I had to chuckle at the dog's sullen expression and asked, "Is this your first dinner there?"

"Yes, but it won't be the last."

"But you didn't get an invitation to her party. Don't get her anything."

"But—"

"Flowers perhaps, but not a lot. I know you, Victor Lennox. You'll want to shower her with fancy cars and diamond crusted collars, but don't fall into that trap. Take it slow."

He let out another whine and tucked his tail, "I guess you're right."

"Before I forget, Richey Denzel wants his brother sprung, and he's not being quiet about it."

Lenox teeth showed again. "Unless it can get delayed until after the election, that hamster is going to stand trial. It can't be helped. With everyone up for re-election, and the female clubs protesting, we'd be fools to try to do anything."

"Scotty's wife is having pups next month."

The pit bull rubbed at his face and jaw. "Why don't they think before they get into trouble? It's bad enough that they do it in an election year, but to get their families involved. I swear that bunch lost their common sense at birth."

"They're also voters, and don't forget the guys are used to being taken care of. It won't take much for them to start talking about the good-old-days or suggesting Reg Calum takes better care of his males."

"Don't talk to me about that weasel." He let out another whine. "Once the votes are counted, I'll do something, but in the meantime, tell Richey that we'll take care of his brother's wife until then."

Richey was waiting for me at the foot of the stairs when I came down. "W-what did he s-say?"

"Nothing is happening until after the election," I said, and watched the hamster's face fall. "Have Scotty's wife send all her bills to Lenox, rent, grocer, doctor, everything. I'll let you know if anything changes."

Richey's face brightened a little, and he smiled. "I-I'll

tell her."

Not wanting to deal with the male any longer, I stepped around him and into the billiards room. Everyone was gone. With nothing left to do, I gathered my coat and hat and left, walking into the sweet fall of rain.

My fingers couldn't find a pulse, and from the coolness of the body, I knew the dog hadn't been dead that long. His head had rolled to the side away from the curb, so I could see his spotted face.

When I looked around, there was no one on the street, and the club was two blocks down. Two males were getting out of an automobile, but otherwise everything was quiet. Several thoughts ran through my mind, but only one remained at the forefront as I slipped into the shadows and headed toward the club.

I slowed my pace, careful not to meet up with anyone until I entered the building. Joe Piper and another amphibian were crossing the foyer from the cloakroom, and they stopped to say hello.

"I hear you had money on Shadow Dancer," said Joe. "How much did you win?"

"Thirty-two hundred."

"Nice, you gaming tonight?" Had I not been distracted by the body in the street, I'd have noticed the higher pitch to Joe's voice sooner.

"Are you all right, Joe?"

The reed frog smirked. "Nothing at all wrong." He then leaned closer and whispered, "I'm going through the change. Do you think the guys will be okay with it?"

"Are you kidding? They'll buy you more drinks and start hitting on you."

He scowled. "I think I'll keep wearing pants and leave the dresses at home for a while. I like free drinks, but if Donny makes a pass at me, I'm socking him in the jaw."

"Might be a good idea, socking the fat weasel that is." We both smiled, and I asked, "Is Victor in?"

"Not sure, we just got here."

I nodded, and we parted company. The attendant said Victor had arrived ten minutes before, and I checked my watch for the time. Ten-fifteen.

Victor Lenox was still in his dinner clothes, sitting at his desk with his hand stretched out toward the telephone when I walked through the door. The pit bull pulled his arm away from the telephone and asked, "How are you doing, Horace?"

"Been better." Closing the door behind me, I stepped farther into the room and sat down opposite Lenox. "How'd dinner go?"

"It was dinner."

I pulled out a cigar and went through the motions, trying to keep my hands from shaking. "Was Ben there?"

"Not for dinner."

"Well, his body is lying in the gutter two blocks down. Do you want me to call the police?"

Lenox didn't seem to hear what I'd said, but he blinked several times before slowly nodding. "Sure."

"The dalmatian was killed, Victor. Are you sure you want me to call them? Do you understand what I just said?"

The dog bared his teeth. "Do you want me to get hysterical? Well, I'm not." A confused expression came across his face before asking, "The police aren't already all over it?"

"No, I just found him. What I want to know from you is, can I let them know I'm the one who found him?"

Lenox waved a hand toward the telephone. "Certainly."

I hadn't realized I'd crushed the cigar I was holding until I reached for the telephone and had to stop to brush the tobacco bits from my hand into the trash. In doing so, I recalled something odd at the crime scene. "Ben's hat was missing." Looking over at Victor, I wondered what he'd really gotten himself into by agreeing to back Senator Jared Wilson Vale.

The coffee I was drinking with the morning newspaper soured in my stomach as I read the account of the night before. If the dalmatian had been anyone else, the article would have been a lot shorter. Instead, the journalists ran with every detail they could find, including the names and addresses of those involved. Speculation stated Ben Vale was most likely the victim of a hold up and that he'd died as a result of hitting his head on the curb after receiving a blow from the front. I was listed as finding the body and calling it in, while the local beat cop had done the same minutes before me. No other relevant information could be gleaned from the article other than Ben Vale had apparently left the house around nine-thirty.

I tossed the newspaper down and shifted in the sleeping sands of the bed. Living in an upscale hotel was a luxury I treated myself to for the last couple of years, and I wondered, with the recent events, if I'd be moving anytime soon.

Rereading the paper, my mind drifted and calculated until a white jacketed waiter knocked and entered to remove the breakfast dishes.

Around noon, I stopped my pondering and headed off to Daniel Pearce's place to collect my winnings. The automatic elevator rattled and hummed all the way up to the sixth floor. The female red squirrel who answered the door to Pearce's apartment was both young and angry.

"Oh, it's you," she said and stepped back to let me in. "If you're looking for Danny, he isn't here. The bum left and took everything with him, even my jewelry."

"What?" I closed the door behind me and after glancing at the female, I looked around the apartment.

"You heard me. He didn't so much as leave a nickel. Momma told me he was no good, and she was right." The rest of her rant was lost in a high pitch run on of obscenities and complaints.

Though I knew what had happened, I still had to ask,

"Did Daniel leave me anything? A letter perhaps?"

With hands on her hips, she said, "No. Why, does he owe you something?"

"Thirty-two hundred and fifty dollars. I won it on a race last night."

"Good luck getting it." She held her hands up. "See these two rings. That's all he left me."

"When did he leave?"

"Last night, I didn't realize it until this morning. But don't you worry, I'm going to make that boar pay." She pulled several pieces of paper out of her dress pocket and shook them at me. When I reached for them, she stuffed them back into her pocket. "You can't have them. They're mine."

"What are they?"

"They're IOUs from Ben Vale, twelve hundred dollars' worth of them, and if you read the paper this morning, you know the dogs dead."

"But since he's dead, those things aren't worth the paper they're printed on."

The squirrel snorted. "They weren't worth anything while he was alive, and that's why he's dead."

Her line of thinking didn't seem right. A collector couldn't get money from the dead, but they could get overzealous during a collection. Was I wrong in my fear that Victor Lenox was involved, or did Ben Vale meet an angry creditor who wouldn't take any more of his excuses?

"Listen, you big lug, that dog owed Daniel money and kept stalling on paying. Last Friday he called Ben with an ultimatum and said he had three days to come up with the money or else."

"You're not just saying that, are you?"

"Why should I lie? Sure, I'm mad, but I don't lie. Why I have half a mind to turn these into the police and have them go after Daniel."

"Where'd you find them?"

"In the safe where else. When I realized he was gone, I

searched everything."

"Do you have any idea when he disappeared?"

"Sometime before nine-thirty, because that's when I got here and was waiting for him to get home. More fool me."

I scratched the scales on my neck trying to fit all the pieces and wondered if Pearce knew something beforehand or if he had something else in mind. "Where would Daniel go?"

The question set off another string of rapid-fire cursing, and I had to wait for a break to ask, "Would he go to New York?"

"How should I know?" Though her words said one thing, her eyes and tail said something else, and I figured she'd realized where the squirrel ran off to.

"Think about what you're going to do. I'd hate to find out you'd changed your mind on calling the police about those IOUs."

"Of course, I will."

The female wasn't going to do anything of the kind.

A drug store occupied the ground floor of the building, and I used the payphone inside to call the Police Department. After getting ahold of the person in charge of the Ben Vale case, I told them what I knew, and that I was making the call because the female was so rattled. I didn't give my name, but I gave them the address, apartment number, name of the red squirrel, and told them to hurry. The last thing I needed was that female skipping town to follow her male before the police talked to her.

The poodle who met me at the door of the Lenox residence smiled and opened the door wide. "Hello, Mr. Avraham."

"Hello, May. Is everyone still home?"

"Yes, sir. They're all still at the dinner table."

"Thanks." She took my hat and coat, and I headed straight to the dining room where Victor and his mother sat facing each other across the table. The third place-setting lay unused.

Victor's mother spotted me in the doorway and smiled. The gray of her muzzle was in sharp contrast to her dark coat. She reached out to me with bony fingers that looked out of place on her thick frame. "There you are at last. Come here and give me a kiss. What have you been up to?"

With a grin, I did as instructed. "Hello, Mom. I've been a bit busy. How's the most beautiful female in the world?"

"Worried about you, you little charmer." It didn't matter that I towered over her, or that I was a lizard. I'd always been her little charmer. "Do sit down and eat."

"Thanks, but I've already had breakfast. Hello, Victor. Where's Amy?"

"She's resting, headache or something."

Stepping around the table, I sat down in a vacant space. "I went to see Daniel Pearce this morning and come to find out the squirrel skipped town with all my winnings. He also left behind twelve hundred dollars of IOUs from Ben Vale. Pearce's lady-friend said he'd told the dog on Friday that he had three days to come up with the money or else."

Victor's eyes narrowed, but he didn't move his tail. "Interesting."

"Mind making me a deputy sheriff, so I can go after him all legal like?"

The dog gaped at me for a minute then asked, "What in the world are you up to now, and why?"

"I intend to get my money back, all thirty-two hundred and fifty dollars of it. If you don't want to help that's great, but if not, I'm going after him, anyway."

"Does this have anything to do with whatever was itching you last night?"

"When was the last time you stumbled over a corpse?" I shook my head. "No, I want Daniel Pearce strung up by the tail. It's not the money, but the principal of the matter.

After a long losing streak, I finally start winning again and that squirrel runs off with my money. Nope, he's not getting away with it. I'm going after him, no matter what, but a badge would make it easier and official."

Lenox scratched an ear. "As much as I don't like you getting mixed up in things, I understand what you're saying. How about making you a special assistant in the District Attorney's office? That might work better."

"If you don't mind," announced Mrs. Lenox. "I'm leaving the table before I say how I feel about what you two get up to." The elderly pit bull picked up several plates and flounced out of the room with her nose in the air. For all her bluster, we all understood she didn't want to hear a word because then she couldn't be called on to give testimony against her only son if charges were ever set against him.

"Can everything be squared away this afternoon so I can get moving?"

Lenox rose from the table. "I'll go make the call now. Do you need anything else?"

"No, but if I think of anything, I'll let you know."

When he left the table, May came in to clear the rest of the dishes, and I asked, "Is Amy sleeping, or do you think I can go up and talk to her?"

"Just took her up some tea and toast, but go on up if you would. The poor pups been crying, but she won't tell me a thing."

"Okay."

Amy Lenox was wrapped in a blue and silver robe and propped up in bed, munching on toast when I knocked on the door. Her eyes were red and the dampness of the fur on her face was evidence that she'd been crying.

"Hello, Horace."

"How's my ankle biter?" I sat down on the edge of the bed and with a flourish, pulled out a cigar. "Will the smoke hurt your head?"

"No, I'm fine."

Her answer had me sticking the cigar back in my pocket. It was bad enough that Victor was holding out on me, now Amy. I tried again. "Sorry, pup. I know it's bad."

"No, really, it's not that bad."

"Since when have I become an outsider?" When she gave me the old puppy dog eyes look, I added, "Ben Vale. Your father may have forbidden you to see the dalmatian, but we both know how hardheaded you can be."

When she didn't say anything, I got up and left. Downstairs, Lenox had gotten off the phone and met me in the foyer. "It's all set. You just need to go over to the District Attorney's office and pick up the paperwork. I need to get to my own office and deal with the sewer contracts. Want me to drop you off?"

Before I could answer, Amy called my name.

"Maybe next time," I said and lumbered up the stairs. Amy ushered me back into the room and closed the door.

"What's the matter with you?" she asked.

"What's the matter with me is that I don't like being lied to."

"But—"

"No, but's, and don't lie to me, or I'm leaving again, and this time I'll make it out the door. When was the last time you saw Ben Vale?"

"Aren't we friends?"

"I thought so until you started lying."

Amy scowled, walked over to the bed, and dropped onto it. "How did you know? Does Dad know?"

"It doesn't matter how I found out, but I don't think your father has any idea."

She let out a whine. "Yesterday afternoon."

I sat down next to her and hugged her while she cried. "Who could have done such a thing? Do you have any idea who?"

I had an idea, but I certainly wasn't going to voice my opinion to her or anyone else. But a few ideas popped into my head at the possibilities.

"You do know, don't you?" she said, looking up at my face. I hadn't thought I gave anything away, but before I could deny anything, she said, "Don't let them get away with it. Make sure they pay. Promise?"

"I can't promise anything. What I can do is catch the person I think might be involved, but punishment is set by the courts and they need proof. If I can get hold of the proof, all the better. Did Ben ever tell you about a squirrel named Daniel Pearce?"

"Other than he was no good."

"The squirrel's into gambling, and Ben owed him money."

"Oh." Amy wiped her eyes with a handkerchief, and said, "I knew there was trouble. Ben had an argument with his father about money and... and Ben said he was desperate. I offered to give him what little I had, but he said it wasn't enough."

"Ben was over a thousand dollars in debt to Pearce, and now Pearce has skipped town. Do you want to help me nab Pearce and bring him back here for questioning and possible charges?"

Her ears perked up and her tail thumped the bedsheets. "What do you want me to do?"

"It's not exactly legal, but—"

"Tell me."

"Can you get me one of Ben's hats?"

Amy stopped her tail wagging and cocked her head to the side. "I don't understand."

"You don't have to. Just get me one of his hats, and I'll take care of the rest. But whatever you do, don't tell anyone about grabbing it, okay?"

"Okay."

CHAPTER 2

The hat I wore while I followed the porter through Grand Central Terminal to the Forty-second Street exit didn't fit. The reason was it wasn't mine. Amy managed to get me the thing, and I was looking forward to putting pressure on Daniel Pearce.

New York was as lovely as ever and welcomed me with a traffic accident. The cab I was in crawled through theater traffic only to be hit by another cab turning against the light on Madison Avenue.

When I switched into another cab and finally made it to my hotel, the clerk handed me two messages sealed in plain white envelopes. Once in my room, I took a closer look at both letters. The first was received at around four o'clock the second just after eight, it was almost nine.

The messages were from David, a rabbit I'd hired to track the red squirrel. He'd not only found her but located her hotel and found out the false name she was using. Apparently, she wasn't the only one with friends in New York because she was running around with a couple of pigeons.

There wasn't much for me to do other than wait for David's call, so I got cleaned up and settled in. David called ten minutes after nine.

The restaurant was just in sight of Broadway, and David waited for me at a corner table. The little black and white Dutch smiled at my entrance, and we shook hands.

"Hello, David."

"They're upstairs in the speakeasy, the red squirrel and the two birds. No sign of Pearce yet, but we should be able to see him come in without being spotted. If he comes in, that is."

"I want a drink. Is there room up there for us?"

"The place is small, and while we might get a booth where the squirrel can't see us, anyone coming in will."

"Let's chance it."

The rabbit gave me a curious glance but didn't ask me what I was playing at. That was fine with me.

"I'll see what's available." He slipped off his chair, disappeared up the stairs, and came back within a few minutes. The rabbit nodded, and we headed up. While we were able to avoid being spotted by the red squirrel, I had a glimpse of her back as she talked to the couple she sat with when we walked to our booth.

David took his coat and hat off, but I kept mine on. The rabbit ordered drinks, and after the waiter left, he said, "If the guy has friends, we're in a hell of a spot."

"Friends or no friends, I'm confronting him as soon as he shows."

While the rabbit sipped his drink, I drank mine.

Daniel Pearce wasn't long in showing up, and when I saw the squirrel, I wanted to break him in two. I got up from the booth and confronted him. "I want my money, Peirce."

If I hadn't had tunnel vision on Peirce, I'd have seen the big ox following him. Getting sucker punched isn't fun, but I calculated that the end result was the same as what I was going for. I didn't bother staying in the speakeasy but made my way downstairs to throw up in the street and expunge all the alcohol I'd consumed.

With the first phase of the plan taken care of, I got into the first taxicab available and headed for Greenwich Village.

Bars in basement apartments aren't unusual, and when they're owned by old friends who haven't seen you in a while, the drinks are free. The waking up on someone's couch with a hazy recollection of what happened the night before reminded me why I'd moved out west.

David was still in bed when I knocked on his hotel room door. He looked at me with bleary eyes and let me in. "You look rough."

"You just look tired."

"I am. After you left, I grabbed your hat off the floor and left. Waiting outside the building seemed a better plan than dealing with that thug following Pearce around. And it panned out. Pearce and his female are at the Buckman over on Forty-eighth Street, apartment 940. With, of course, a false name. I hung around until three and knocked off."

David gave me the name Pearce was staying under, and I asked him if he had a gun.

"Sure, it's in the drawer." The rabbit yawned, stretched, and reached for his pants. "What are you planning?"

"Confronting Pearce. Go back to bed, I'll handle it."

"You're the boss," he said, and planted his face in his pillow.

I retrieved the gun from the drawer, checked to see if it was loaded, and dropped it in my pocket before heading out.

The Buckman was a large apartment building that took up the entire block. Inside, I gave my name to the clerk, and he called ahead to apartment 940 before sending me up. Daniel Pearce answered the door with a smile, but not the kind you use for a friend. The squirrel had enjoyed watching me get pummeled by the ox and was looking forward to gloating over the situation.

"Good morning, Avraham. How are you feeling?"

"We need to talk."

"We do? I would have never guessed. Come on in."

Pearce led me into a large suite where both the female red squirrel and ox were busy packing. When they spotted me, their smiles were just as cruel, and the ox cracked his knuckles and licked his lips in anticipation of another round.

"I need to talk to you, Pearce. Is there any reason you

need to have your clowns along?"

The ox didn't seem to register the insult, but the female let out a string of curses. Pearce waved her off. "Say your peace or leave."

"Fine." I took off my coat and hung it over the back of an easy chair. As for the ill-fitting hat I'd retrieved from David, I stuck that behind me before I sat down. "The money can wait. I'm here on official business as a special investigator for the District Attorney's office."

"My, you've come up in the world." Pearce's smile faltered, but his eyes stayed on me. "Don't tell me you came all this way to talk to me about Ben Vale?"

"Yes, I did."

Pearce pointed a thumb at the red squirrel. "Why do you think we're packing up? She told me about your frame up, and about how you sent the police after her about those IOUs. If the dumb broad hadn't led you here, I wouldn't have had to move."

"Dumb broad? Why you—"

"Shut up and pack." Pearce glared at the sow and I wondered what the two squirrels saw in each other before deciding I didn't want to find out.

"She gave us a line on you, and we're following it up."

"Do I have a warrant out for my arrest?"

"Not that I know of."

"Then I suggest you leave and don't come back."

I rose, took a cap out of my pocket, and grabbed my coat. "Be seeing you, Pearce." As I left, it was to the shrieks of laughter of two squirrels and an ox.

Outside the building, I turned the corner and nearly barreled into David. "What are you doing here?"

"Last time I checked; I still work for you."

"Well grab a taxicab. Those three are leaving, and we'll need to tail them."

The rabbit bounced off but returned quickly with a taxicab. "Do I want to know what you did to set them scurrying?"

"Later."

We watched as the trio exited the building and climbed into their own taxicab. Then we followed them to Forty-ninth Street where a row of old brownstones stood. When the squirrels entered one of the houses, I told David, "Stay here. If I come out with Pearce, you'll have to find your own taxicab and wait for me at the Buckman."

"And if you don't."

"Use your own judgment."

Ignoring any other questions, I slipped out of the vehicle and headed straight to the house the squirrels entered. The door may have been locked, but it was easy enough to push open. When the door slammed shut behind me, I was ready for the ox.

The few punches the male was able to score didn't hurt near as much, and I could hear Pearce laugh and egg him on. At least until I managed to get the gun from my pocket and shoot the damn ox in the leg. Nobody was laughing then.

"Be thankful I didn't bite you." While the ox wailed like a calf, I pointed the gun at Pearce. "Let's go for a ride." I had no idea where the female was, but I wanted to get out of there before frying pans or other items started flying at my head. As it was, a lot of noise came from upstairs, but nobody came to see what was happening.

The squirrel proceeded me out the door, and I kept my hand on the gun, though I hid it in my pocket. Pearce's tail looked like a cleaning brush it was puffed out and shaking so bad, but the male was a coward when he no longer had the upper hand.

David left the taxicab as we walked over and got in the back. "Drive," I said. All the time the old nag at the wheel stared forward, and without a word, did as he was told.

"This is a hold up?" said Pearce.

"Have you forgotten I've come up in the world?"

"But you said I didn't have any warrants out for my arrest."

"What, and you believed me?" Laughing more for effect than mirth, I added, "You're going down for killing Ben Vale."

"But I didn't do it. Yeah, I told him to pay up, but I figured the IOUs were worthless. That's why I took off with your money. There's no way you can pin his murder on me. Even my female will back me up."

"Remember the hat I was wearing, Pearce? Didn't you think it odd that it didn't fit me? That I left with a cap instead of a hat?"

Pearce blinked. "Maybe."

"When we search your old hotel, we're going to find Ben Vale's hat stuffed down in the recliner. Now, you have a choice. You can fry for killing the dog, or you can give me back my money right now, and I'll make sure I'm the first through the door when the police search the place."

To emphasize my point, I stuck my snout in close and smiled, showing teeth while my tongue tickled his fur. "Deep fried squirrel sounds tasty."

The squirrel's eyes were so big, they almost engulfed his head, and it took a minute for his voice to work as his jaw moved.

Pearce broke down, babbling out the most outrageous excuses for what he did along with impossible to keep promises. When he finally calmed down enough to give me an address, we set out to go retrieve my money.

CHAPTER 3

I stepped off the train from New York feeling great all the way from the concrete steps connecting the train-shed to the street level waiting room. Once outside and before I got in a taxi, I bought a newspaper. The half-column spread on the front page had me worried.

The article stated that a deer named Jason East was gunned down the night before just blocks from where his brother was killed. None of the witnesses could identify the males in the black touring car in which the shooter rode, but several bullets were fired. Eight of which ended up in the deer's body. Neither his remaining brother nor fiancé knew of any enemy's the deer had.

If Richey Denzel hadn't been pestering Victor Lenox about springing his brother Scotty out of jail, I wouldn't have thought anything of it. But since the hamster was sitting in jail after having run down Eric East during a bootleg run, I didn't like the coincidence.

The first thing I did was try to get hold of Lenox when I got home. When that didn't pan out, I called the District Attorney's office and made an appointment.

District Attorney Robert Nadel was a plump brown mouse who waxed his whiskers into a fashionable curl. The large walnut desk in his office was clear except for a telephone and a heavy green desk set decorated with a nude holding an airplane.

Nadel shook my hand, welcoming me into the room and nearly pressed me into the leather chair in front of the desk. "How was your trip?"

"It was all right. I just read in the newspaper about Jason East. How is that going to affect your case against

Scotty Denzel?"

The mouse never could look me in the eye and squirmed as he talked. "Shouldn't make a difference at all. We still have the other brother to make the identification." Nadel glanced up at me. "Why? Is there something I should be worried about?"

"Just wondering. But as long as the last brother's willing to talk, everything should be fine."

"Sure." Nadel looked away, and his whiskers did a series of twitching before the mouse excused himself for a moment and left the room. I pulled out a cigar and smoked while I waited for him to come scurrying back into the office. "I just had to check on things. We've been a bit busy lately. Sorry about that."

"No problem. Anything on the Ben Vale killing?"

"Nothing yet." The mouse fidgeted behind his huge desk. "Thanks for bringing Daniel Pearce back. The case against him his pretty flimsy, but his skipping town on the same night doesn't look good for him."

"That squirrel blew town because I won a very large bet, and the greedy little furball decided to run off with my winnings instead of paying up." When the mouse stared up at me in surprise, I had to chuckle, and said, "Victor didn't send me after him, he let me go."

"So you don't think he did it?"

"No, do you?"

The taste in the air held more than Nadal's usual nervousness, and he fidgeted some more before pulling an envelope out of a drawer, setting it on the end of the desk. The envelope's address was type written as was the three questions inside.

Why did Victor Lenox steal one of Ben Vale's hats? What happened to the hat Ben Vale was wearing the night he was killed? Why is the lizard who claimed to have found Ben Vale's body, now working in your office?

"That came today," said Nadel. "We always get crazy letters every time something happens. It's just that... well I thought you should see that one."

Nadel didn't object when I stuck the paper back into its envelope and put it in my pocket. From the look in his eyes, he was worried and so was I. The thing looked very similar to one of the envelopes in the stack of mail I had at home but hadn't bothered to open.

Before the mouse could say another word, the telephone on his desk rang, and he picked it up. "Yes? What? He can't do that. The whole case rests on him." By the time Nadel hung up the phone, he was shaking. "Charlie East won't testify against Scotty Denzel. The deer's now saying he's not sure who was driving the truck that ran his brother down."

The mouse ranted, and I let him, but when he turned to me and asked, "Did Lenox…?" I had a sinking feeling that things were heading south and fast.

"No. Lenox had no intention of springing the hamster before the election. Both Richey and Scotty understood this."

"Sorry, I was just… I didn't realize." Nadel apologized again, and I managed to get out of his office with an invitation to lunch.

Richey Denzel was a foreman and was standing beside a row of males operating a nailing machine at the box factory. When he spotted me, he waved and stepped over. The smile on his face seemed forced.

"Hello, Richey." I pointed a thumb at the door. "Let's get out of this noise."

The hamster nodded, said something that was lost in the din of the place, and walked outside. The platform we exited onto had a wooden stairwell that led twenty feet to the ground.

"Do you know that one of the witnesses against your brother is dead?"

"Y-yes. R-read it in the n-newsp-paper."

"The other ones not sure if he can identify your

brother."

"R-really?"

"Yes, and if he doesn't testify, Scotty will be free. What's the matter, Richey? Is there something wrong?"

The hamster's eyes darted all over, and he pulled at his fingers.

"Did you go see the East brothers about Scotty?" The male nodded and switched to chewing on his nails. "What happened, Richey? Did they refuse to back down? When was this?" He still refused to meet my gaze, but the little rodent held up three fingers, indicating three days.

"Hope you have an alibi."

"I-I do. I-I-I was at the c-club all night. Eight o'clock t-till t-two. The g-guys can t-tell you." Richey named three different people who were at the club, but while I figured the male hadn't pulled the trigger, Richey understood he needed an alibi.

I tried calling Lenox from the payphone at a restaurant down the street but still couldn't get a hold of him and left a message. From there, I headed back home and checked my mail. Amidst the pile of unopened letters was a white envelope with a typed address.

Inside, the questions read, Was Ben Vale still alive when you met him or was he dead? Why did you wait until after the police found the body to report it? Why frame the innocent and let the guilty go free?

Examining both my letter and the District Attorney's, the letters were the same all the way down to the postmark.

For the next hour, I read and re-read the notes and smoked until the telephone rang. Victor Lenox finally returned my call.

Lenox arrived at my place with a smile. "When did you get back?"

"This morning, and the good news is that I got what I went after. Did anything happen while I was away?" I grabbed a couple of cocktail glasses and made us both a drink.

"Nothing much. The sewer contract is straightened out, and since we can't chance making any money off it, we'll make it up next year with the street work and extensions."

"Was there a memorial or something for Ben Vale?"

"The burial was Friday."

"Burial? Even with all his money, I thought the Senator would have opted for a memorial instead of rubbing his wealth in everyone's eyes. The processing plants charge a lot to give up good meat."

Lenox shrugged. "No one seemed to mind, and there was a good turnout at the funeral."

"You were invited?"

"The Senator suggested it, yes. I spent most of the afternoon with him."

I gave him a quizzical look, and he said, "Yes, Wendy was there as well."

"First name's now. My, you're running fast. Does she know what your intentions are?"

Lenox let out a growl. "Am I on a witness stand?"

"No, but you might end up on one. Did you hear about Jason East being dead and now Charlie East refuses to testify against Scotty Denzel?"

"Who? Oh him, what of it?"

"Damnit, Victor, think with your head and stop sniffing around the Senator's daughter. Since you refused to help Richey Denzel get his brother off the hook for running down that deer, the hamster went to Reg Calum for help. When threatening Jason and Charlie East didn't work, he had Jason gunned down. I'm guessing that weasel did something to put the frame on Richey for the shooting because the hamster was at the club the entire time. Since he never stays that late unless it's a special occasion, he knew what was going down."

The pit bull blinked several times. "What are you getting at?"

"Think about it. Calum made it appear like you either arranged the hit or are providing an alibi to a killer. The people you've been bowing and scraping to here lately aren't going to like that. As for those who do know what happened, it's looking like you're no longer willing to take care of the guys. If they want protection, they'll have to go see Reg Calum for that."

Lenox growled. "I wish the election was over."

"This wouldn't have happened if it was, and right now I'm not sure what we can do about it."

"Well, I do. I'm having the police bust every one of Calum's gin joints."

"Bad move. The dog's in blue aren't used to enforcing Prohibition in this town, and they're not going to like it. You're using a sledgehammer on a framing nail."

"What else can I do. I go for the frontal attack; I've never been a planner like you. So unless you can come up with something, I'm running Reg Calum out of town."

I sat near the wall in a comfortable chair, smoking a cigar as Lenox talked to the eight other males and two females of various species in the room. The campaign was going well, but certain districts still couldn't get the votes they needed for our side.

A knock on the door had me standing and answering it. The kangaroo on the other side looked rattled. "Reg Calum's downstairs wanting to see Victor."

There was no need to repeat the message, because everyone in the room heard the kangaroo and looked at Lenox.

"Tell Calum I'm busy," said Lenox. "If he wants to wait, I'll see him when I'm done here."

"You heard him," I told the kangaroo and closed the door. Wanting to observe the others at the table, I didn't sit down right away. From the looks on each of their faces, I could tell which ones weren't happy with the current feud with the weasel, and the taste of the air confirmed my suspicions.

A half-hour later, Lenox rose from the table, dismissing the meeting, and shook everyone's hand as they left the room.

"Do you want me to go, Victor, and leave you to deal with Calum?"

"No, stay."

Calum didn't knock when he came into the room, but the weasel entered with a sense of arrogance followed by one of the largest alligators I'd ever seen.

"Hello, Reg," said Victor.

"Hello, Victor. I've a bone to pick with you. I've paid my dues, but I'm getting shafted."

"Sounds like you have a problem."

"Yes, I do. Half the dogs in this city are getting paid by me, but instead of protecting my places, they're raiding them. Imagine my surprise when I find out from Captain Hawking that the order came down from none other than you."

"Perhaps you weren't paying them enough, and perhaps Hawking needs a nice vacation."

"Business is business, and politics is politics. Keep them separate." The weasel barred his teeth at Lenox, but the big dog just smiled which seemed to infuriate the weasel more. "Listen you mutt, I've paid my protection money, and I'm opening Dust Bowl tonight. Understand?"

Instead of answering, Lenox picked up the telephone and dialed. "Chief Levy, this is Victor Lenox. I've heard on good authority that Reg Calum is reopening the Dust Bowl tonight. Make sure it's shut down and stays down." After he thanked the Chief and hung up, the pit bull glared at Reg Calum. "You're through here, understand?"

"This isn't over." The weasel turned on his heel and stormed out the door followed by the alligator.

When all was silent again, Lenox asked, "What do you think, Horace?"

"That you made a wrong move."

I set aside a few shirts that were too worn to bother with and sifted through another pile, while two maids busied themselves packing my trunks. When the doorbell rang, one of the rats stopped what they were doing and answered the door. When Lenox stepped into the room, he looked around and asked, "Are you planning a trip?"

"Yes."

"Can you spare a half-hour?"

"Sure." Turning to the rats, I said, "Get as much as you can packed. The rest will have to be shipped later along with everything else."

Once outside on the street, we walked down a block where the entrance to a speakeasy was located down an alley. We headed inside, took the hallway down to the bar, and were shown into a small narrow room.

"Are you leaving for New York," asked Lenox.

"Haven't decided yet. Just away from here. I'm tired of this place."

"You mean me. This is a hell of a time to abandon me, Horace. Lord knows I'm not the easiest person to get along with, but neither are you."

Neither of us said a word as the bartender came in, set our drinks on a small table and left.

"Are you sure you want to go?"

"Yes, and I'm going."

Lenox let out a low whine before pulling his checkbook from his pocket. He wrote out a check, fanned the ink dry, and set it in front of me. "Take it, I owe you. Hell, I owe you a lot more."

"I don't need your money, Victor."

"Take it."

The dog wasn't happy, but neither was I. We were both too stubborn for our own good, so I picked up the check and put it in my pocket.

"It won't do any good, I won't stay."

"Then tell me how I handled Calum wrong."

"Why? You didn't want to listen the first time."

"Tell me anyway."

"Fine." Taking a drink, I arranged the words before I spoke. "Reg Calum will fight because you've given him no choice. The weasel is backed into a corner with nothing to do but play the long shot. If the election is lost, he still has a toe hold in the city. If he can't upset things, he's gone anyway. That weasel has no chance but to go up against the cops, and that means a crime wave, and a crime wave just before elections is a bad thing."

"Should I have put him down or let him run free?"

"You should have left him a line of retreat."

Lenox scowled and shook his head. "I don't understand anything about your way of fighting. When someone's cornered, I take them out. The system has always worked for me in the past."

"Just because it worked then, doesn't mean it'll work now. Things change, Victor, and you need to adapt. Especially with what you want to go after. Frontal attacks don't work with the crowd you're courting."

Lenox let out a low growl, and I finished my drink. "I need to get going."

I got up from the table, but before I made the door, Lenox grabbed my arm. "Wait."

I was already angry at the dog's blindness to the situation, and his insistence on wanting me to stay only added to the fuel. "Take your hand off me."

"Horace—"

"I said take your hand off me."

The next thing I knew, I was taking a swing at him. My fist connected with his heavy jaw, and the only thing it did was have him look at me in surprise. That, and have the dog ready for an attack. Both of us stood our ground. With a hissing monitor lizard and a growling pit bull in the room, no other sound in the place existed.

No one moved.

My frustration and anger had dissipated with the blow,

while it took a moment for Lenox to calm down. When he did, he burst out laughing. "You're insane, Horace. You know that?"

"No, but I think I broke my hand on your face. What's it made out of, concrete?"

The dog laughed again and hollered for the bartender to bring us another round.

CHAPTER 4

When I considered how much stuff I had packed, I decided to have breakfast in bed. The interruption should have been expected, and Pat Bloom had the manners to knock first.

"Cushy. Very cushy," he said.

"Have a seat," and I pointed to a chair. "What brings Reg Calum's right-hand male to my door?"

The iguana put a cigarette in his mouth and lit it. "There are a lot of boxes in the other room. You moving?"

"I've been thinking about it."

"Where too? Back to New York, maybe?"

"Thinking about it, though the destination hasn't been decided yet. Possibly I'll try one of the other big cities for a while. If you're wondering about me returning here, it's quite unlikely."

Both of us stared at each other unblinking to the point most mammals would have fidgeted and filled the room with chatter or grown bored and left. But we were lizards. Slow shouldn't be mistaken for calculating.

Bloom broke the silence. "Why don't you talk to Calum before you leave?"

"Why? We've never been friends, and I doubt he'd shed any tears if I didn't say goodbye."

"That isn't the point. The point is, you two could do a lot of business together."

I downed the rest of my, now cold, coffee and moved the tray to the side. "Doubtful."

"Isn't it at least worth listening too?"

It didn't seem likely that Bloom would force the issue,

the odds weren't in favor of that, even if he had a gun. Which I was sure he did somewhere on his person. If there was a fight, biting would be both uncivilized and obvious. There weren't that many large lizards in this town, and Bloom was too big to worry about the toxins in my bite. Though I might have been able to give him a nasty infection.

"Why would Calum want to do business with me, or rather why would I want to do business with him?"

Bloom's rumbling laughter sounded more like a motorboat running on bad gas. "Everyone in town knows about the bust up you and Lenox had the other day. Since Calum's got plenty of dough to pass around, he thought you might like some before you blow town for the big city. Who knows, he might make it worthwhile for you to stay."

"Doubt that, but I guess it won't hurt to hear him out. Mind leaving the room while I get dressed or do you like to watch?"

Reg Calum rose from his chair and nodded in greeting when I walked through the door. The weasel didn't offer to shake my hand, but he did motion to several comfortable looking chairs. "Take your coat and hat off and stay awhile."

The chill in the room, I attributed to the early morning and the fact that Calum hadn't bothered with a fire. Mammals don't mind the change in temperature as much as cold-blooded species do, but I thought it best to be sociable and removed my coat and hat.

"I owe you for trying to talk Lenox out of—"

"You owe me nothing, Calum. What I told him, benefitted him. Lenox will understand his decision was a bad move before this is all over."

Calum nodded, he in his chair, and I in mine. Neither of us were in a hurry, but as with most mammal–lizard conversations, the weasel spoke first. "How much did Bloom tell you?"

"Only that it might be to my benefit that I talk to you. Monetarily anyway. And before you ask, yes, I've split with Lenox. Even have a one-way ticket out of town in my pocket. Bloom can attest to everything I own being packed up."

"You're originally from New York, aren't you?"

"Does it matter?"

"Not particularly. Honestly, I don't care if you came from some podunk town in the middle of nowhere. What I care about is doing business with you. Ever thought of getting back at Lenox?"

"Not until Bloom showed up at my door. Why?"

Calum nodded again. "You've been with Lenox a year, two?"

"Almost two."

"And you've been tied to the hip for most of that time. Hell, he welcomed you into the family and everything. That's got to burn, how he chucked you over."

"If you think you're giving me an opportunity to make trouble for him, you're not. That's something I can do at any time I wish."

"Okay, then let's treat this as a business venture." The weasel smiled and tented his fingers. "What if, after the election, I gave you a gambling house that you could run as you like?"

"That'd only be good if the election goes your way. If not, it's an empty proposition. Guarantees are a safer bet."

"Good point. How about ten grand now, and if we win the election and beat Lenox, ten more, plus the gambling house?"

"So you want me to turn on him?" A stiff ache creeped into my fingers, and I wondered about the weather outside. It was still early in the year, and winter was still a couple months off.

"I've got one of the mice from the newspaper outside right now waiting for the scoop, but you'll want payment first." Calum pulled a stack of bound bills from a drawer in an end table and set it on a low table in front of me. "Let me call him."

The weasel put his fingers in his mouth and let out a loud whistle after which a harried white mouse scurried into the room with pencil and paper in hand. The journalist was virtually salivating as he smiled at me with crooked teeth.

"Tell him all about the sewer contracts, why Lenox killed Ben Vale, and the Ridgeway debacle."

"The sewer contracts angle is a bust, why risk making waves before an election. As for Ridgeway, not only was that a while ago, but I'd hate for upstanding people like myself to be roped into things beyond their control and get blamed for things they didn't do."

"Perish the thought." Calum smiled as he talked. "And the rest?"

"If you don't mind, I'd like to have this conversation in a more comfortable environment. Your place is downright cold." Truth be told I was having trouble thinking it was so chilly.

"No, you're staying here." The weasel let out another whistle and a pair of thugs burst through the door. I tried rising, but my body resisted any quick movements. "Put him in the cooler for now, we'll work him over later. Get the ice out from under the floorboards. My feet are freezing."

"Shut up, you clown," said the stork.

The alligator at the table with him rapped his knuckles on the wooden surface between them. "Leave him be and play your hand. If the guy tries to leave again, we'll have more fun. Otherwise play."

The mattress on which I lay was bare of any sheets. My body no longer ached from the cold of ice hidden within a small room, but the beating I'd received. Someone had wrapped my mouth shut to keep me from biting anyone, and I briefly wondered if I had tried to do so or if someone was just taking precautions.

The room was relatively bare, and other than an open door leading to a bathroom, the only other door was closed in the windowless room.

I'd gone in knowing the odds, and the gambler in me couldn't resist trying to take the bet and turning it to my advantage. But the weasel was prepared, and I was trapped. If I didn't get out, I was dead. With my eye on the door, I managed to get to my feet. The pair at the table didn't move but watched as I stumbled to the door, collapsing as I reached for the knob.

When I tried again, the alligator was by my side and knocked me back to the floor.

"Don't hit him too hard, or you'll kill him," said the stork.

"It's fine, this guy's tough. I think he likes it."

Somehow my brain registered the rattle of a doorknob, and Reg Calum and Pat Bloom stood over me. The weasel and iguana looked down at me before Calum looked over at the alligator and stork. "Have you two been beating on Avraham for fun?"

"He has," said the stork. "The fool keeps trying to escape. I've seen some hardheaded people in my day but, this guy takes the cake."

"Well don't kill him just yet. Clean him up. I'd like to talk to him."

The alligator and stork dragged me into the bathroom and dumped me into the tub. The hot water from the tap was both a blessing and a curse. The warmth seeped into my body yet scalded my scales. From there, they pulled me back into the room and sat me back on the bed. The wet rag tying my mouth shut was removed, and Reg Calum sat across from me in one of the chairs.

"Avraham, can you hear me? You're going to give us all the dirt on Victor Lenox and don't think you won't because we're going to beat on you until you do."

Other than glaring at him, I hissed. When I attempted

to bite the little weasel, someone clocked me one and the darkness of unconsciousness returned.

No one was in the room with me when I came to, and I got up to try the door again. Stumbling around as I was, I must have made a horrible racket because the alligator barged in and nearly flattened me to the floor.

"Knock it off, I'm trying to sleep here."

When I tried again, the thug came in swinging, and I woke up to Pat Blooms ugly mug. The iguana helped me back to the bed and said, "Would you use your head. These two mugs don't have the brains to fill a whiskey glass. They're going to kill you."

"Let them." At least that's what I think I said.

Sometime later, Calum and the others came back into the room to go over the same old questions. When I refused, I got another beating.

The next time I woke up, I staggered into the bathroom for water and ended up collapsing on the floor. Despondency as the odds tipped further away made me attempt suicide when I found the small broken half of a pair of grooming scissors under the sink just inches away. Unfortunately, the blade was too rusted and dull to do little more than scrape my scales.

Still, I thought I could use it somehow and slipped the thing into my vest pocket. When I did, my fingers brushed the lighter I always kept in my pocket. The realization that Calum's males hadn't removed everything from my person had me smiling, and in my head, I could see the scales tipping back in my favor.

Staggering back out of the bathroom, I shredded the mattress, placing the pieces at the foot of the closed and locked door of my prison, before eventually pulling the entire thing over. One of the thugs had left a newspaper in the room, and I tore and crumpled the paper before lighting the pyre. It took me three attempts to get the lighter to light, but when I did, I ended up with a nice blaze with a lot of smoke.

The noxious air sent me back into the bathroom to soak a towel in which to wrap my head before going back to the door, crumpling to the floor exhausted. The ruse worked, and the enraged alligator pushed through the door grabbing me by the collar. The guy hauled me out of the room, cursing me every step of the way before shoving me into another, locking the door.

Somehow, I kept my feet underneath me and almost broke out in hysterical laughter when I saw the windows. I crept forward like a sinner to the alter and nearly banged my head on the wall when I lurched forward the last few steps.

A brief moment of panic seared my nerves when I tried opening the windows, and they wouldn't budge. Relief came when I tried the locks, and the sashes moved. Outside the window the world was dark, but that didn't matter. With fists gripping the windowsill, I slipped out of the room feet first, belly scraping the brick wall. When my feet found no purchase and the weight of my body strained my hands and arms, I let go, and fell into the darkness.

CHAPTER 5

Someone was touching my face, and the air tasted of gardenias and antiseptics. I managed to crack an eye open and a pretty doe in a white uniform peered down at me.

"Where am I?" My voice sounded like sandpaper even to my own ears.

"St. John's Hospital."

"What day is it, month and year?"

The doe smiled, touched my cheek, and said, "You've only been here three days, and it's Monday."

"Where's the telephone?"

When I tried to get up, she pressed me back down into the bed with little effort. "None of that. There'll be no using the telephone or getting yourself excited."

"Call Victor Lenox then, I need to talk to him."

"Mr. Lenox is here every afternoon. While I doubt the doctor will let you talk to anyone yet, I'm sure he'll be here in the next few hours." The nurse checked her watch and nodded before looking back down at me. "Now, will you please calm down. You've done too much talking already."

"But I need to talk to Victor now."

"The doctor will be here soon to check you over, though I doubt he'll let you speak to anyone."

"But—"

"That's enough. Now, do what your told."

"Didn't anyone ever tell you the best patients argue?" When she didn't respond I added, "Did anyone tell you what happened to me?"

"I'm guessing drunken brawl; now would you stop fussing and let me check your scales."

Victor Lenox arrived early that afternoon. The pit bull

smiled, and his thin tail kept wagging uncontrollably the entire time he was in the room. "Thank god you're alive." The dog held my unbandaged arm. Only when I felt the warmth of his hand did I realize the temperature in the room and notice the heat lamps and wall thermometer.

"I'm fine, but you've got to grab Richey Denzel and take him over to—"

"We've already done that. Don't you remember?" I must have given him a blank look because his smile got wider, and he patted my arm. "The morning you were brought to the hospital, you were thrashing around hissing and batting everyone with that thick tail of yours, refusing to calm down until you talked to me. Only then would you let anyone work on you."

"Did I? I don't remember a thing."

"One of the orderlies said your tail was like getting hit by a baseball bat, but everyone kept well away from those teeth of yours. Anyway, as soon as I got here, you told me about Denzel and Braywood, then passed out."

"Guess I've got some apologizing to do. Did you get Denzel?"

"Yes, the hamster was picked up and identified along with that big alligator who hangs around Reg Calum. Two others were also identified, but I don't know their names. Richey Denzel is in jail, and the alligator is in hiding, but we don't have proof that will put Calum away. Not even a parking ticket."

"I thought I could trap the weasel. That's the only reason I went to see him. Only he'd set a better trap for me." I stopped talking, trying to piece together my memories, but there were great big gaps in places. "Strange, everything is all muddled, and I can't place everything. I remember it being cold, and I couldn't think. The beating, and fire."

"You were certainly a mess when the beat cop found you crawling down the street on all fours and trailing blood. He said you looked like something out of a nightmare."

The nurse with the big doe eyes popped her head in, and I couldn't resist saying, "Peekaboo, I see you."

She giggled and came into the room. "I just wanted to make sure you were awake enough to see visitors. Mr. Lenox is here, and he's brought a lady to see you."

From the twinkle in her eyes, it couldn't have been Lenox's daughter, and there was only one other female I could think of that would promote that much awe. "Wendy Vale?"

"Yes." The doe nodded, and I frowned.

"Can you tell them I'm asleep?"

"Considering they can hear you grumbling, no."

"Only senator's daughters, never a governor's daughter or even a president's daughter. What's wrong with me? Aren't I pretty enough?"

"There's been a policeman guarding your door day and night fighting off all your adoring female fans." I couldn't miss her sarcasm as she smiled, and said, "Now behave, and I'll send them in."

She booped me on the end of my snout and smiled before exiting and automatically checked the thermometer on the wall on her way out.

I closed my eyes briefly, tasting the air, as I let my mind do the calculations of possibilities.

Wendy Vale came into the room with her face a mask of casual politeness, wearing a dress which complimented her spotted fur. "Hello, Mr. Avraham, I'm glad you're doing well, and I hope you don't mine me imposing on you. Since you're Victor's best friend, I just had to see you and make sure you were all right."

"Much obliged. Please, pull up a seat," I said, and motioned to one of the chairs near the bed.

"We can't stay long," said Victor, who'd followed Wendy Vale into the room. "I have meetings to get to."

"You can't stay, but I can," said the dalmatian. "That is

if you don't mind?" She'd said the latter to me, and I nodded.

"Sure, I don't mind."

Lenox came around the bed and moved the chair closer for her to sit. There was a smile on his face, and his tail kept wagging. The pit bull checked his watch, and said, "I need to get going. Is there anything I can get you before I leave?"

"No, everything's fine, thanks," I said.

"As for the meeting, it's with Hoffman. How far do you think I should go?"

"Don't be direct with him. Anything straight forward scares him, so as long as you take the long way around in the conversation, you could probably get him to commit murder if you wanted to."

Lenox chuckled. "The railroad vote is all that's needed. I doubt anyone needs to get murdered over that." He grew serious and said, "But I do wish you were up and about."

"Don't worry, I will be in a couple of days. Did you get a chance to read the newspaper this morning?" When he shook his head, I looked him square in the eyes. "Someone's done a lot of talking, and the newspaper ran a six-week list of the crime spree, starting with Ben Vale. The list for arrests is considerably short and make the police look incompetent."

Wendy Vale let out a whine when I mentioned her brother's name, and Lenox gave me a warning glance I decided to ignore.

"The newspapers were especially vocal about Ben Vale's murder and how the police are deliberately staying away from the case and not investigating. Not to mention my going to New York to pick up Daniel Pearce. They're trying to twist that into a nice political conspiracy."

Lenox's ears were down, and his tail was still. I expected his teeth to show at any moment, as I barreled on about the article. "They're accusing the police of raiding places that won't fork over campaign contribution money instead of protecting them like they'd been doing for years. There's a promise of a list of places that did pay."

The dog wasn't happy. Lenox nodded, crammed his hat on his head, and said his goodbyes, promising to pick up a newspaper.

Wendy Vale and I sat in silence for a while before she asked, "You don't like me, do you? Can I ask why?"

"What makes you think I don't, or is it my bad manners? Everyone gets a taste of those."

"Well, I'd like you to like me, because you're Victor's best friend."

"Politicians have a lot of friends, and Victor is a politician."

The dalmatian eyed me for a minute. "Victor thinks you're his best friend, and I think you are too. Otherwise you wouldn't be in this hospital right now, having done what you did."

I couldn't quite keep the smile off my face. She was a smart cookie. "That dog picked me up out of the gutter when no one else batted an eye. I'm not good around your sort. Society people."

She nodded and rose from her chair. The female didn't say goodbye as she left, but when the nurse came in to check on me, she gave me a questioning glance.

David came to see me. I hadn't seen the rabbit since New York and gave him a smile. "Hello David."

"Other than the bandages, you don't look so bad."

"That's because I have scales instead of fur, there's nothing to shave off, and I'm still in one piece."

David sat in the chair next to my bed and lit up a cigarette. "How's the food here?"

"They refuse to serve me decent carrion, saying that I could get sick if it's not fermented right. Hospitals are goofy. They tell you to stay while serving you food that makes you want to leave. But that's not why I sent for you."

I reached under my pillow and pulled out the envelope I'd hidden there and handed it to David. "Another job, and one that needs discretion. That one I received here at the hospital. There were others. One at my home, and I know the District Attorney has received one. He's probably gotten more by now. All type written with no salutation or signature, but always three questions."

The questions in this letter were: What was Reg Calum so eager to learn from you about Victor Lenox? Does it have anything to do with Ben Vale's murder? Why were you so determined to keep it a secret, if it wasn't?

David read through the letter and examined everything. "Any ideas?"

"No, but I want to find out who's sending them. I got rid of the others, but there all the same. Keep that one, but be on the lookout for more. I can't be the only one getting these things."

"Everything's the same, but the questions differ?"

"Yes, but they're all pointing to the same thing. Who killed Ben Vale?"

The rabbit put the paper back into the envelope and tucked it into his pocket. "Is there a possibility that Lenox is connected with the dalmatian's murder?"

I didn't answer right away because it was a question I myself had asked for some time. In the end I said, "No."

The nurse came in holding a huge basket stuffed with fruit and a couple of jars of pickled eggs and insects. The doe set it down on the side table. "Isn't this nice?"

While I nodded, she pulled out the card and sniffed it. "I bet it's from you-know-who."

"What are you willing to bet?"

"Anything you wish."

I studied her a bit, looking for a tell, and realized she was too confident. "You've already peeked at the card.

That's cheating."

"It's not cheating, it's getting the upper hand." She handed me the card, and I read it. A single word was written in a feminine hand. "Please."

"Well, you win. Take as much of that stuff as you want and make it look like I'm eating it."

That afternoon I wrote a thank you note. It took me a couple of tries even with mulling the words over in my head.

I was up, sitting in a chair, wrapped in a robe with feet encased in bathroom slippers eating breakfast and reading the newspaper when Amy walked into the hospital room. "Well now, isn't it the ankle biter. What are you up too?"

"Why didn't you come visit me when you first got back from New York?"

"Sorry, but I was a bit busy, then ended up in here."

"You could have at least called." She gave me those pained puppy dog eyes of hers, and I wondered for how long what little innocence she had would remain. She'd already seemed to age several years from the last time I'd seen her. "Well?"

I laughed. "You look good in that outfit."

"Would you be serious? Will they hang Daniel Pearce for Ben's murder?"

The mutt got to the point, that was for sure. "Doubt it. There's not enough evidence, and personally, I don't think he did it."

She scowled at me. "Did you think… did you know he didn't do it when you asked for my help to… to fix him up?"

"Of course not. Who do you think I am?"

"You did know it." The accusation surprised me. I'd always thought of myself a decent liar even among other lizards. Her eyes were cold and angry. "You only wanted to get back the money that squirrel stole from you, and you tricked me into helping you."

She clutched at her handbag in a way that threatened to

rip it in two. "Do you know who killed Ben? Was it my dad?"

"I hope you're asking if your father knows anything about it."

"I'm asking if my father killed Ben."

"Keep your voice down. Whatever gave you that idea? And why would he?"

When I reached for her, she stepped away, but at least she kept her voice down when she asked, "Did he?"

Keeping my anger in check was difficult, but I managed not to snap at her. "If you're going to go around acting like a silly twit, would you mind keeping your voice down? Idiotic notions are a dime a dozen, but your father doesn't need to have you running your mouth."

"He did kill him, didn't he?"

"No, he did not, and the sooner you get that ridiculous idea out of your head the better."

"If he's innocent then what does it matter what I say?"

I couldn't believe what I was hearing, or that Amy could be so stupid. If anyone heard Victor's own daughter accusing him of murder, it wouldn't matter if he had a thousand witnesses who said otherwise, he'd be deemed guilty by public opinion.

"You'd be surprised," I said, letting my anger seep into my voice. "You're still young, naive, and have no idea the lies that plague politics, let alone life. Now, where did you get ahold of such a crazy idea?"

The pup shrugged and said, "Nowhere, I just… saw it."

"From this morning's newspaper?"

"No."

At first, I didn't believe her, but then I remembered the typed letters. I held out my hand and demanded, "Give me the letter. I want to see it."

"What?"

"The letter. You're not the only one getting typewritten letters with three questions. Hand it over now."

Amy looked away as her ears lowered. "How'd you

know?"

"Like I said, you're not the only one receiving anonymous letters. Everyone in town has been getting them, and by your reaction, this one is probably your first. Am I right?"

She nodded, reached in her purse, pulled out the note, and handed it to me. The letter read: Are you really so stupid as to not realize your father murdered your lover? If you didn't know, why did you help Horace Avraham frame an innocent person? Did you understand that by helping the guilty you become an accomplice?

"All the letters have been the same." I crushed the thing and tossed it in the waste basket. "Now that you're on the instigator's list, you'll get more."

I stopped and studied her face. Amy was still so young and naive, and I understood why Victor sheltered his only daughter from the world. I wondered if it was only delaying her pain or compounding it.

"Reg Calum is trying to stir up trouble for your father. He even tried paying me for any dirt I could give him, and why? Because I had an argument with your father. When I refused the weasel's offer, I ended up here. And the only reason I didn't end up buried in the woods somewhere was because I escaped."

"What did you fight about?"

"That's nobody's business but our own."

"It was about Ben, wasn't it? You found out he killed Ben, didn't you?"

"Oh, for the love of... Make up your mind. Did I know all along or did I just find out?"

Amy shuffled her feet, but her tail stayed between her legs. "Why did you ask if I read the newspaper? What's in it?"

"More of the same nonsense your spouting." I pointed to the newspaper I'd folded and sat on the table when she'd come in. "Read it if you want. They'll be more of it until the election, and it'll get worse."

I stopped talking as she picked up the newspaper and read. The poor pups body shook as she reached the end. "They wouldn't print it if it wasn't true."

"Truth doesn't sell newspapers, and believe me, the garbage written is going to get worse. Politics is a rough game, and people can get very nasty during a campaign." I pointed again to the newspaper she let drop back on the table. "The porcupine that owns that newspaper isn't worried about the truth or anything that will hurt your—"

"Liar, I know Mr. Patel and went to school with his wife. She was only a few years ahead of me. He wouldn't write anything untrue."

The laughter that burst out of my throat I couldn't help, and it made the dog jump back. "That porcupine is in debt up to his eyeballs. The mortgages on both Edgar Patel's house and business are owned by The City Trust Bank which belongs to the opposition candidate running for senator. Patel has no choice but to run what he's told or risk losing everything."

There was nothing in Amy's demeanor that what I was telling her was getting through, but I went on. "This trash is going to get worse, but you shouldn't let it get to you. Victor knows it's playing dirty, he's a politician—"

"He's a murderer."

"And you're a fool."

"He's a murderer."

"This is insane. Your father had nothing to do with Ben Vale's murder."

"I don't believe you. I'll never believe you again," she barked before turning, bolting from the room.

When she left, I stared out the window in thought, rolling an unlit cigar around my mouth. Someone truly hated Victor Lenox. Picking up the typed letter from the trash, I read it again, and stuffed it into my pocket before going back to the paper.

The newspaper claimed to have affidavits tucked away in their safe regarding information about the dalmatian's murder and listed seven different items, mostly regarding Victor. From his quarrel with Ben Vale about Amy and their sneaking around to see each other in a secret love nest, to insinuating a second argument happened the very night the dog died so close to the club Victor owned, and the fact no police officer investigated the crime.

The article ended with a long-winded rant about bringing justice by using the newspaper to tell all, and the article was signed by none other than Edgar Patel, owner and publisher.

I dropped the thing into the waste basket, lit my cigar, and thought.

Victor's mother visited me early that afternoon with a warm smile followed by hugs and kisses. Tired of nothing but sleeping and sitting, I stood while the elder dog took a seat.

"You're looking well, though not your best. How are you feeling?"

"Just peachy. The only reason I'm putting up with this place is the nurses. Nice legs, every one of them."

"Yes, you would. Do sit down, your making me nervous."

I did as I was told and smiled as she said, "Victor said you did something very noble to end up in here. I wish you two would behave."

"Aw, Mom."

"Don't, aw mom me. I have a serious question to ask you, and I want the truth, so look at me while I ask it. Did Victor kill Ben Vale?"

I stared in open mouthed surprised at the dog in front of me before saying anything. "No, he's innocent. Why… what… Not you too?"

"I didn't think he did. Victor's always been a good pup, but with all the horrid rumors I've been hearing, I just needed to hear something positive. I don't understand politics, and honestly, I don't want to. Such a nasty business."

Taking both her hands I smiled. "I'm glad someone believes in him. It's nice to know that someone besides me believes in his innocence. And it's especially nice that it's his mother."

I was writing another thank you note to Wendy Vale for a package of four books when David hopped into the room smoking a cigarette.

"Got something, but I'm not sure you're going to like it."

There were a lot of things I didn't like lately, but sticking my head in the sand wasn't going to help any. "If it has to do with what I hired you for, then I'll like it plenty."

The rabbit looked from his cigarette to me then sat in a chair the furthest distance from where I sat in the room. "It's looking like Victor Lenox's own daughter is sending those letters."

Such news coming after what happened already hit me hard. "Are you sure? How did you find out?"

David got up, took several papers out of his pocket, and handed them to me. Each were identical and had the same things typed on their surface. "One of those is the original you gave me yesterday, the other a fake I typed up. There's no difference."

The rabbit took another drag on his cigarette. "That article in the newspaper gave me the idea, so I headed over to Charter Street where Ben Vale rented the place he and Amy Lenox would meet. There was a Corona typewriter along with a stack of paper and envelopes in the apartment, and as far as anyone knew, only two keys for the couple. The female has hers and she's been back to the place a few times since Ben Vale's death."

I didn't know what to say, so I didn't say anything as David headed back to his seat and sat down. "The police got there before me, but luckily I knew one of the dogs, the one in charge, in fact, and for a ten spot he let me poke around."

"Do the police know about what you found out?"

"No, I didn't say anything, but there's no telling what they might find out from another source. I didn't get anything out of my friend, other than they're posting a guard for now."

"What kind of place is it?"

"Apartment thirteen twenty is a single room with a bathroom rented to a Mr. Smith. Real imaginative. The lizard who runs the place said she didn't know who they were before the police showed up. Do I believe her?" David shrugged and went on. "The pair were there a lot, mostly afternoons, but the pit bull came back a few times after the dalmatian's death."

"And?" I could tell by the look in his eye there was more.

"She probably wasn't the only female who'd been up to the apartment. I couldn't get the building supervisor to confirm one way or the other, but it wouldn't be too hard to get into the building and upstairs without anyone noticing. That and the building supervisor acted shifty. Yeah, I think Vale was seeing other females beside Amy Lennox."

"Could you tell from what was in the place?"

"Not really. The only female things that were there was a kimono, toiletries, and pajamas."

"What about a hat?"

"No hats."

Leaning back in my chair, I stared out the window to think before saying, "Thank you, David. I might have another job for you soon, but that will be all for now."

"Anytime."

After the rabbit left, I got up, headed to the closet, and grabbed my clothes. I was fully dressed by the time the nurse came in to check on me.

"Why aren't you in bed?"

"Because I have to go out."

"You can't go, the doctor hasn't released you yet, and it's raining out."

"I'll borrow an umbrella." I kissed her on the cheek and slipped out the door.

CHAPTER 6

Mrs. Lenox opened the front door, and her eyes grew wide as her ears perked up. "Horace, what are you doing out of the hospital, and on a night like this?"

"Don't worry, Mom, I took a taxi. Is Victor or Amy in?"

"Victor left about an hour ago, probably to the club, and I haven't a clue as to where Amy's gone off to. Do get in out of the rain."

"No, I've got to find Victor. I'll check the club."

"Nonsense, you're in no shape to be running around on a night like this. What did you do, walk out of the hospital?"

"Sort of."

The pit bull scowled at me, but then her eyes softened. "Is it about Victor? Is something wrong?" Fear crept into her eyes, and she said, "You mentioned Amy."

"I need to find them, but don't worry. It's not as bad as it could be." I hugged her, soaking up her warmth. "If Amy comes home, make her stay, but don't let on to either of them that you know something's wrong."

I walked a few blocks with a borrowed umbrella to a nearby drugstore to use the payphone. First to call a taxi and second to call Edgar Patel of the newspaper. Neither of which I wanted traced back to the Lenox house.

Failing to contact the porcupine that ran the newspaper, I called up David. The rabbit was in. "Hello David, Sorry to interrupt, but I need to find out if the female we talked about went to see Edgar Patel. If she did, where'd she go afterwards."

"Are you talking about the newspaper guy?"

"Yes."

"Don't know, but I could find out and check back with you at the hospital."

"I'm not in the hospital, I'll be at home. Get the information quick as you can, but be quiet about it, okay? If I don't answer the telephone, keep trying."

"You're the boss."

We hung up, and I headed outside and got into the waiting taxi. We'd driven to the first address I'd given him when a thought occurred to me, and I gave the beaver driving another address, and we changed directions. When we arrived at a squat gray house, I told the driver to wait and got out of the vehicle.

District Attorney Robert Nadel didn't answer the door, the vixen maid did, but the mouse didn't keep me waiting. He scurried into the reception room. "Avraham, how nice to see you. Please, let me take your coat and hat."

"I can't stay. I just got out of the hospital and heading home. Is there anything new happening?"

"No, nothing. The two males that, um…" The mouse waved a finger at me. "Well, we haven't caught them yet, but we will, don't worry."

"It's not like I died. The best you can do is charge them with assault. Did you get any more of those letters?"

The mouse refused to meet my eyes. "Y-yes, one or two maybe."

"How many?"

"Three."

When Nadel tried changing the subject I asked, "Were they all along the same line?" When the mouse didn't answer right away, I leaned over to peer into his eyes. "Did they all accuse Victor of killing Ben Vale?"

Nadel nodded but kept his mouth shut while he shook with fear.

"You getting a case of the nerves, Nadel? Has Victor noticed?"

"No, no, I'm fine."

"Sure. Have you found out who's writing the notes?"

"We have a line of inquiry, but it's too soon to say. There might be nothing too it."

The air tasted of fear, though the mouse tried to sound friendly. "You've found the machine the notes were typed on and where, so you have enough to guess."

The mouse nodded, stopped shaking, and hung his head.

"Well, you can't go wrong with taking things slow. Rushing things can lead to mistakes. I'm feeling tired, so I'll leave you to whatever you were doing. Good night."

The District Attorney brightened at my words and smiled. "Thanks, Horace."

I was sitting at home in front of a nice warm fire when I got the telephone call around nine o'clock. The rabbit had found where Amy had gone off to, and it meant I'd have to go out again.

Right after I hung up, Victor called. We talked for a bit, and I told him I was feeling tired and was going to go to bed. I wasn't feeling sociable.

Bundling as warm as I could, I exited my apartment and walked the half block through the pouring rain to the garage. There, a lanky tomcat in filthy overalls met me with a smile.

"What are you doing out on a night like this?" he asked.

"I need a car, something that will get me over the country roads tonight."

The cat's ears pivoted forward, and his eyes dilated, but his tail made no movement. "Hell of a night to go traveling those roads. I've got an old Buick that should work, and I don't much care what happens to it none."

"Fill the tank then. What's the best road up Lazy Creek way in this weather?"

"That depends how far you're going."

I didn't really want to tell the tomcat my destination,

but there was always a chance he could guess. "Where it runs into the river."

"Patel's place." He smiled, and the white of his teeth made his coat look dingier. "Depending on your destination, directions matter." When I nodded, he said, "Take the New River Road as far as Evert's place, then go over the bridge along the dirt road if you can and take the first crossroads east. That'll get you to Patel's place along the top of the hill. If you can't take that route in this weather, take the New River Road and cut back on the Old River Road. And don't worry. I didn't see your crazy tail on a night like this and don't know where you went."

"Thanks."

When he had the car ready and I slipped in the driver's side, the tomcat said, "There's an extra gun in the side pocket."

"Gun?"

He gave me another toothy grin and said, "Pleasant trip."

The clock on the car's dashboard said ten-twenty-five when I reached the hill. I wasn't looking forward to walking out in the rain, and not for the first time wondered if I shouldn't have just pulled into their driveway.

I got out of the vehicle and half walked, half slid down through the foliage and underbrush toward the patches of light that shown through the trees. Beacons in the night directed me to where the cabin stood. My pace slowed the closer I got, but I forced myself to keep moving and made it to the door.

Edgar Patel answered my knock. The bespectacled porcupine peered anxiously at me, but I kept my head down until I was inside. "Come in out of the rain. This is a terrible night to be out. Are you all right?"

"Car trouble." Once inside, and the door closed I raised my head to glance around. The cabin wasn't really a cabin and more of a lodge with its large living, dining, and multiple guest rooms, but it was furnished in a rustic style.

Amy Lenox stood up from her place near the roaring fire to glare at me as Edgar Patel took my coat and hat.

"Mr. Avraham, I didn't expect to see you out here, and on a night like this." By the sound of his voice, Patel was worried and scrambling to keep everything in order. When he looked over at Reg Calum, I half expected every quill on his back to fall out.

The weasel lounged on a comfortable chair and smiled lazily at me. The alligator and stork next to him needed no introduction. I'd felt their fists one too many times not to be on a first name basis.

The alligator smiled, his rumbling laugh filling the room. "Look who's back for more fun. Couldn't get enough of me beating on you, could you?"

"Shut up, Tom, you talk too much," said Calum while keeping his genial smile.

The stork didn't say a word but kept an eye on me. A pretty porcupine in a red dress was the person I hadn't met before, and I lumbered slowly into the room to introduce myself.

"You must be Mrs. Patel," I said, and took her hand. "How nice to meet you. I'm sorry for the interruption, but my car broke down and, in this weather, well, it's not fit for lizard or mammal."

"Please, do sit down by the fire and warm yourself." I did just that and waited for the stiffness to leave my fingers and limbs. Edgar Patel fidgeted but sat down as silence descended on the party.

When I was sufficiently warmed, I turned to Amy and said, "Hello, ankle biter." A glare is all I received in return, and I half expected her to bite me.

Mrs. Patel seemed like the safe bet to talk to, and I smiled at her. "Amy here said you were schoolmates."

I kept an eye on Calum's crew and nodded to them. "Didn't expect to see you here, aren't the cops looking for you?"

"Just thought we'd play it safe. You in the hospital and

all. People go there to die more often than not, and I'd hate to have my guys bothered prematurely." Calum waved his lit cigarette in my direction. "Looks like you're feeling just fine."

"Pretty good."

"Good." The weasel looked at the alligator and stork. "You two can go back to town in the morning. An assault charge isn't nothing."

"Don't forget, the one is still wanted for the murder of Jason East. The alligator did gun the poor deer down in the middle of the street. And that won't bode well for Mr. Patel here. Harboring a fugitive, I believe it's called."

"I didn't know they were here." The porcupine's voice was at least an octave higher than it normally was. "I mean…" He looked at Calum. "You know you're welcome here, Reg, but all I'm saying is that where the law is concerned, I had no idea that anyone was here until we arrived today."

"Yes," said Calum. "You just helped us without knowing about it."

The weasel's eyes remained steady as the porcupine fidgeted, and it was Mrs. Patel who finally broke the silence. "It's been frightfully dull until you arrived."

"Dull?" I asked and moved to sit on the floor in front of her with my back to the fireplace.

"Yes, very dull. When Edgar asked me if I wanted to come up here with him and Amy, I thought it would be fun. But when we arrived, his friends were also here, and ever since, they've been hinting at some secret they don't want to share. Amy's been just as bad." The female didn't bother to keep the irritation out of her voice. In fact, I didn't have to taste the air to understand the room was thick with tension.

"Now Cindy." Edgar's voice trailed off when his wife gave him a steely eyed glare, and the porcupine studied his nails.

"Don't even start, Edgar, you know I'm speaking the

truth. Whatever business you planned on talking about hasn't happened, and I can only assume it's because I'm here. And believe me, if it wasn't for the weather, I wouldn't stay one more minute in this place."

I noticed Amy's ears twitch, but she didn't look up.

Cindy Patel turned her attention back to me and asked, "Did you really break down, or are you just here for their silly meeting?"

"Can I lie and say, yes, because after seeing your lovely face you're much more interesting than they are."

"Perhaps, if you really did change your mind."

"And I promise I won't be mysterious about anything. Don't you have an idea of why everyone's here?"

The female shrugged. "Not really, but it's probably something stupid and political."

"Smart cookie, and right on the mark." I glanced around the room to make sure no one was going to try to stop me from spilling the news before talking. "Amy thinks her father killed Ben Vale."

Amy whined and her ears lowered, but everyone else kept quiet as Cindy Patel looked at the dog in astonishment. Edgar Patel resorted to chewing his nails as Calum glared at me.

"She actually—"

"Stop it," cried Amy. "Stop it, Horace."

I stared down at the pit bull using every lizard trick in the book until she sat back down and lowered her eyes. "Isn't this why you're here, Amy? Isn't anyone besides you and your father's enemies supposed to talk about it. Who cares about the truth or that your accusations will ruin your father's reputation?"

"He murdered him," whined Amy.

"See what I mean?" I looked at Cindy Patel. "After seeing that load of garbage your husband printed in the paper this morning, Amy here went to him thinking her father really did kill the dalmatian. Oh, I know that Edgar doesn't believe Victor killed the dog. Your husband is in a jam with the house and business mortgage to the hilt to City Trust Bank which is owned by Calum's candidate for the Senate. So he has to print what he's told and—"

"Now, Avraham, you really—"

"Let the lizard talk, Patel. I'd like to hear what he knows."

The porcupine looked like he was about to fall apart while the weasel sneered.

"Thanks," I said and turned back to Cindy. "Where was I, oh yes. The ankle biter here, Amy, she went to your husband looking for proof, but of course he doesn't have any. If he did say Victor killed Ben, he knew it would be a flat out lie because all he's doing is slinging mud where he's told. That's why he brought Amy up here to the cabin, to hide her up here until the morning papers go out. And what will the headlines be, but Amy Lenox accuses Father of murder, or some such thing. All nice and neat in black and white served up with the morning coffee."

Cindy stared at me with wide-eyed horror on her face, and I wondered how pristine she'd thought her husband really was. From the look on her face, he was apparently fool enough to keep secrets from her.

"I have no idea if Edgar knew about Calum and his thugs being here, and I don't care," I said. "And Amy came with him willingly, so it's not kidnapping. Or would that be dognapping? No matter, as long as she can't tell anybody what she was up to until after the damage was done."

"Finished?" asked Calum.

"Yeah."

"Great, it's our turn to give your side a blackeye, and we're doing it up just swell. The female came in on her own with her own story, and we ran with it. With a present like that all tied up in a bow, who wouldn't use it to their advantage? Now if you don't mine, I need to get some shuteye, and I suspect everyone else around here does too."

"What have you done, Edgar?" Cindy's voice was low, angry, and held something else I couldn't place.

"Darling, there is plenty of evidence to demand the police investigate—"

"That's not what I'm talking about." The female's eyes bored into her husband, and he shied away.

Cindy and I stayed downstairs while everyone else headed upstairs to the various rooms. We sat before the fire, me for warmth, smoking a cigar, and she, looking with tragic eyes at the burning log.

The stairs creaked, and I heard Edgar Patel's pleading voice. "Darling, won't you come to bed?"

When she didn't answer, the porcupine called my name. I turned to glance at him with an uncaring expression, and he wandered back up the stairs.

Sometime later, Cindy Patel spoke. "There's whiskey in the cabinet. Would you mind pouring a glass?"

"Sure. Straight?" The female nodded, and I got up and rummaged through the cabinet for both the bottle and glasses. I made us both a large and gave her a glass. Her eyes were too bright, and her smile crooked. Part of me wondered what else Edgar was hiding. What thing did he promise her that went snake eyes to the point where her finding out ended everything? Part of me was glad I didn't have a clue.

"What should we drink to, my husband?" she asked.

"Hell no. Why not to you?"

She raised her glass. "To me." The female did a good job of downing the drink.

"You might want to eat something with that."

"No, I want it this way."

"Suit yourself," I said as she held out her glass for me to refill.

"How about we use the bench?"

I followed her instructions and moved away the chairs so that the bench seat was in front of the fire. When she told me to turn off the light, I knew exactly what she was up to, but I did it anyway. The odds were in my favor.

We sat next to each other on the bench, and she leaned into me. Careful of her quills, I put my arm around her.

"To you, this time," she said when we refilled our glasses.

The creak of the stairwell announced we weren't alone before we heard the plaintive, "Darling."

I couldn't help chuckling when she leaned into me and said, "Throw something at him, will you." My rumbling laugh was cut short as she kissed me.

We hadn't got very far when we heard the shot, and I jumped out of her arms.

"Where's his room?" Cindy blinked at me in dumb terror as I repeated myself. "Where is Edgar's room?"

"In the front."

I bolted up the stairs and nearly plowed into the alligator who was fully dressed but for his shoes. "What's going on?" The male tried to stop me, but sleep and being in a cooler area of the lodge slowed him down and let me slip past, leaving his question unanswered.

Reg Calum came out of his room and was right behind me.

When I flung the door open to Edgar Patel's room, I stopped dead in my tracks. The lamp lit Edgar's body which lay on the floor, his mouth open and seeping blood. From the position of the body and the gun by his side, it was obvious what the porcupine had done. A bottle of ink was open on the table with a pen next to it atop a piece of paper.

While Calum knelt and checked the body, I edged over to the table and pilfered the paper without looking at it and crammed it in my pocket.

Though it was a large room, having me, a weasel, an alligator, and a stork wearing only what god gave him all crowding the room, was making me claustrophobic. Calum stood. "The coward shot himself through the mouth."

I got to the door and met Amy staring wide eyed into

the room. From the look on her face, she could smell the blood. "What happened?"

"Edgar Patel shot himself. Get dressed, I'll sit with Cindy until you can get downstairs to be with her. She'll need a friend."

When I got downstairs, I wasn't sure if Cindy Patel had passed out from the alcohol or fainted with the realization of what happened. The female lay still on the floor unmoving, but her breathing was clear. Other than putting a pillow under her head, I dared not try touching her for fear of her quills.

Using the dying firelight to read the note I'd pulled from Edgar's desk, it only took a few lines to figure out what it was. The handwritten will left everything to his wife and appointed The City Trust Bank as executors. He may as well have let them foreclose on everything and saved a bullet for all the good it would do him. Besides, I couldn't let them bury Victor. I quickly shredded the paper, tossing the pieces into the fire and making certain the fragments burned to ash.

That done, I moved back to the female and attempted to wake her without getting impaled by her quills.

By the time Reg Calum and his crew got dressed and came downstairs, I was in my raincoat and hat and heading for the door. "Where do you think you're going, Avraham?"

"There's no phone here in the cabin, so I'm going to go find one."

The weasel nodded and stepped away from the stairs. "That's a great idea. Only there's something I want to talk to you about."

I didn't see a pistol, but I wasn't taking any chances either. I pulled mine from my pocket and moved so that the weasel and the other two could see it while shielding it from the two sobbing females now on the couch. "I'm in a bit of a hurry, Calum, so make it fast and without any funny business, Okay?"

He didn't blink but stayed where he was. "There's an open bottle of ink on the desk and a pen on the table. Looks like the porcupine was writing something, but we can't find anything. Don't suppose you spotted anything?"

"Bad eyesight is a discussion for later, after I come back."

"Better to do it now."

"Don't worry, I won't be long." I backed toward the door and got out of the place as quickly as I could. Thank goodness the rain stopped, but I still had the worry of Calum's goons finding me before I found a phone. Staying off the trail and keeping to the brush, I made my way through the woods in the direction of the car. I could hear them in the darkness searching for me.

When I reached the road, I didn't find the car, but neither did I hear my pursuers chasing after me. I'm not sure how long I walked along the road before spotting the shadow of a house, its clean lines contrasting the trees against a star lit sky.

I made quite a racket as I barreled into the low fence. Once I found the gate and unhooked the latch, I staggered to the door. I thought about using the butt of the gun instead of my numbing hands to pound on the wood paneling, but when I raised my hand, I was no longer holding it. Somewhere along my trek through the woods, I'd lost the fool thing. My hands would have to do.

From somewhere on the second floor a voice called out from an open window. "What's with all the racket down there?"

"Horace Avraham from the District Attorney's office. I need to use your telephone to report a dead body."

The scrape of wood signaled the closing of a window, but it still took an age for the person inside to open the door. The goat that answered stuck his nose in my face and asked, "What's all this about a dead body?"

"Telephone, now."

"You look a mess. What's the number and I'll—"

"Just show me where it is and leave me alone."

The goat might have protested, but considering I nearly fell on him, he grabbed hold of me, guided me through the hallway, and sat me in a chair next to the thing. "Private," I said, when the goat reached for the receiver. Other than scowling, the male let me be.

I called Victor Lenox and waited a dozen rings before the dog picked up on the other line. "Hello?"

"Victor, it's Horace. Shut up and listen. Edgar Patel committed suicide up at his place and didn't leave a will. The porcupine was up to his ears in debt, so the courts will have to appoint an executor. Understand?"

The dog swore and said, "The newspaper."

"Exactly, but that's only part of the issue. Make sure it comes up in front of the right judge so that they stay out of the fight until after the election. But right now, you have to stop the morning issue from going out with the dynamite it's loaded with. An injunction from the judge should do it. You'll have to wake him up, do it quick. There's not a lot of time, three maybe four hours tops."

"What are you going to do?"

"I'm going back to the Patel's cabin. Amy's there, and I'll need to bring her home. Don't ask, I'll tell you everything in detail when I see you." We hung up, and I tried making it to the front door without falling but couldn't manage it.

The old goat was at my side, helping me up. "Let me get you to the davenport, and I'll get you a blanket."

"No, I need to get back to Patel's. Can I borrow your car?"

"You're in no shape to—"

"Then I'll walk it."

"And people say we goats are stubborn. Hold on to your britches, and let me get my coat. I'll drive you."

When we drove up to the porcupine's cabin, everything was quiet. Amy and Cindy Patel were sitting on the floor, but Calum and his thugs were nowhere to be seen.

"Where's Calum?" I asked.

"Gone," said Amy. "They left right after you did."

Cold and exhausted, I fell to the floor.

CHAPTER 7

Senator Vale smiled, put his napkin on the table, and said to his daughter, "Do you mind if Victor and I go upstairs to my office? We've a few things to discuss about the election."

"Can Mr. Avraham keep me company?"

Both dalmatians looked at me, and I nodded. While Victor and the Senator headed for the stairs, Wendy Vale lead me from the dining room to a sitting room across the hall. The black dress she wore complimented her spots, but she wore no jewelry.

Someone had lit a fire in the fireplace, and I moved closer. "Do you play?" I asked, motioning to the piano Wendy Vale stood next to.

"Yes. Not very well though." She pulled at her fingers, and I suspected would have chewed her nails if she were alone. "How is Amy?"

"It's been a least a week, but she's fine, from what I understand. Why?"

"Victor said she had a nervous breakdown."

"Oh, that. I'm surprised Victor didn't tell you all about it. Amy's fine, she's just got it in her head that her father killed your brother, so he grounded her until further notice. Or at least until she stops trying to shoot her mouth off to anyone who will listen."

"She's a prisoner?"

"Last I checked, she's still a minor and sending a pup to their room when they're out of line is still considered an appropriate punishment."

"Oh." The dalmatian sat down and put her hands in her lap. "Why would she think such a thing?"

"A lot of people do. First off, it's politically advantageous to those who oppose your father to have Victor arrested for murder. The Senator can't get re-elected without him."

"Who would believe them without evidence?"

"A lot of people. It doesn't take much." Her manner had me curious, and I wanted a few answers to something that was suddenly nagging me. "Someone's been sending anonymous letters to people."

"Oh, yes, I've got one just today. Would you like to see it? That's something I wanted to talk to you about."

"No, that's okay. The letters are all on the same vein. The newspaper tried taking what little information they had about your brother's death and smearing Victor before we managed to stop them. They might have been able to have him executed just on popular opinion."

"Is he in any real danger?" The dog was trying hard not to let her tail wag, but she couldn't stop it from quivering.

"If your father loses the election, and if Victor loses his hold on the city and state governments, there's a good chance, yes. But if your father wins, no one will go after Victor."

"Do you think he'll win?"

"Yes."

"Then he'll get off scot-free for murder."

The laughter which rumbled up out of my mouth I couldn't stop, nor did I want to. "Should I call you Judas?" When her ears flattened and her tail lowered, I knew I had her. "Let me guess. When the police returned your brother's items, you took the key to his little love nest in order to type up all the anonymous letters. You're the one stirring up all the trouble and set Amy against her father. Did the Senator make you string Victor along or was it your idea?"

She bared her teeth, and I nodded. "I'll take that as the Senator made you do it, or maybe I should say you went along with it. That dog doesn't care a wit about his offspring or anyone else. But then you already knew that, didn't you? Hence the letters. I warned Victor against backing him, but he was, and still is, in love with you."

I stepped closer and leaned down so I could look her in the eye. "Do you hate Victor that much? Even if I can prove his innocence, would you still hate him?"

"Yes, I can't stand the male."

"So, you hate him, therefor he must have killed your brother."

"No."

"Have you said anything to your father?"

The dalmatian barked a laugh. "You said yourself he doesn't care for anything but winning the election."

"And he would know if Victor killed your brother." She bared her teeth again, but I went on. "Did Victor say anything that night about Amy and Ben?"

"Don't tell me you don't know everything about that night?"

"I don't. Mind telling me what you know?"

"It didn't have anything to do with them." A noise outside in the hallway startled her, and we heard Victor and the Senator's voices. In a low tone she said, "Can I talk to you tomorrow?"

"After ten in the morning, my place."

Wendy nodded just as the two males entered the room.

Victor was in a good mood when we left Senator Vale's house and got into the sedan. "I'm glad to see you're getting along with Wendy."

"I said I'd try. There's something I want to discuss with you tomorrow, but I'll need to confirm a few things first. Will you be at your office?"

"Yes, it's the first of the month, and I need to get a few things done."

"How's Amy?"

"Not pregnant, thank god. Do you think... you know... her and Ben?"

"Who knows what pups get up to at that age, but it's

not like the Senator kept a leash on his son. Try not to think about it."

When we reached the club, Victor headed to the office, and I joined a game of poker.

Wendy Vale didn't show up to my apartment until almost noon. "Sorry I'm late."

"Don't worry about it. We didn't have a set time, anyway." When I ushered her into the living room, she did the typical dog thing and wanted to smell every corner. Once I gave her the grand tour, I asked, "Are you satisfied no one else is here, or would you like to check the closets?"

Her ears tucked back briefly. "You're a gentleman. I'm sorry if I was a bit too curious."

"I'm nowhere near being a gentleman. I'm just a gambler and politician's hanger-on."

"Let's not quarrel with each other. I wanted to tell you about what happened the night Ben was killed."

Motioning to a seat, I lit another cigar and sat down. "Tell me what you wish. The only thing he told me was Ben wasn't home."

"Ben was home, just not at the dinner table. He refused to eat with us because of the situation with Amy and was supposed to go out to eat. Victor, my father, and I were the only ones at the table. Afterward, my father left us alone in the sitting room and… and Victor grabbed me and kissed me. It was absolutely appalling."

"Didn't he give you any warning?" I managed not to laugh, but I couldn't help smiling.

"What? No, I don't think so. It was all I could do to sit through dinner and not show any animosity toward him. Why?"

"Like I told you yesterday, I warned Victor to stay away from you and your father. Either that or make sure everything was signed, sealed, and delivered before the election. Your father was using you as bait to get Victor to help him win the election, but then, we both knew that. So what happened after that?"

"Nothing, I ran upstairs and, on the way, I met my father and told him what happened. I was furious and told him it was his fault for bringing Victor into our home. I heard the front door and assumed it was Victor leaving and went to my room, but not before I spotted Ben on the steps above us. That was the last time I saw my brother alive. My father came to my room and told me he was gone."

After she sniffled a bit and pulled out a handkerchief, I asked, "And?"

"And what? Don't you see? Ben was so mad he left the house without his hat and ran out after Victor, and Victor killed him."

"Nope, not buying it. Pitbull's don't have the hair trigger most people think they have. Victor knows his own strength and has spent a long time keeping his temper in check. Trust me, I've fought alongside the dog. No, he wanted to marry you, so that would mean keeping a cool head while talking with your brother. He'd have spent all his energy calming the pup down. If there was a fight, Ben's body would have looked a lot different. Though I suppose it could have been accidental or self-defense."

"Then why didn't he report it?"

"Like I said, he wanted to marry you." I tapped my cigar ash into a tray. "Victor didn't kill Ben."

"He must have. There was no reason for Ben to be anywhere near Victor's club or on that street. Plus, he didn't have his hat."

"Didn't your father see Ben leave? Does he feel the same as you do?"

"Why wouldn't he have? And why shouldn't he feel the same. Victor Lenox killed my brother." Tears built up and threatened to spill down the fur of her face. "You should know. You found Ben."

"While I found Ben's body, nobody was around when I

did. What I reported to the police was everything I knew. But let me tell you one thing I do know. Your brother was no angel, and had I known what he was getting up to with Amy and a bunch of other females, I would have castrated the runt."

Wendy stuck her nose in the air. "Males will be males."

"Don't give me that malarkey. If you really believe that, you're as deluded and stuck up as your father. I understand that you want to remember the good in your brother, but don't go so far as making him a saint."

"Victor Lenox killed my brother."

"On that, my dear, we'll have to disagree."

When Wendy Vale left my apartment, I called Victor's office. The dog wasn't in yet, so I had to leave a message about being in later. I ended up staring out the window thinking and smoking a cigar until the telephone rang. Joe Piper was on the other end. The reed frog sounded worried and wanted to meet. I told him to give me half an hour.

Once we hung up, I snubbed out my cigar and walked several blocks to get some food into my stomach before heading over to the hotel Joe was staying at. Taking the elevator up to the fourth floor, I got to chat with the otter who operated the thing about the race that afternoon. He didn't like my pick.

Joe Piper was in room four-twenty. When he opened the door, the green dress and bonnet of flowers he was wearing gave me pause. "Is it Mardi gras?"

"What?" Joe looked down at himself. "Oh, it does clash with my spots doesn't it."

"Just a bit. Might want to lose the garden as well. Otherwise you're looking great. Can I start calling you Josephine yet?"

"Sure, but come on in." Joe looked around the hallway, hurried me inside, and closed the door. "Things don't look to good, Horace. With Gordon going down to City Hall, I feel like I'm in a jam."

"Gordon who? Mind starting from the beginning, I'm a little lost."

"Yeah, right. Well, you remember the night Ben Vale got knocked off?" Joe patted down his dress as if looking for something. Since the thing didn't have pockets, and the frog was acting jumpy, I assumed he was looking for his cigarettes. I picked up the pack sitting on a side table, handed him one, and lit it for him. "Thanks."

"What about the night Ben Vale died?"

"Gordon and me, we saw Victor fighting with the pup underneath the trees."

"But you got into the club before me," I said.

"I'm talking the first pass. Gordan and I was supposed to pick up Shelly, but he wasn't there when we knocked on the door. So we left and drove back to the club."

"Are you sure it was them? It's dark in that area, or do you have night vision?"

"Pretty sure. It's hard to miss Victor."

Something still didn't make sense, and I said, "Tell me exactly what you saw. Every detail. Victor didn't have the pup down on the ground, did he?"

"No, no, nothing like that. You know when two people square off and you can tell their having an argument without touching each other. That's what I mean."

"And Gordon went to City Hall with this?"

"Yeah, and now Nadel is looking for me. I'm thinking I should leave town on a long vacation. This is crazy, and I don't want any part of this. What do I do if they nab me?"

"Let them," I said. "The best thing you can do is talk to the District Attorney and tell him you're not sure who you saw and that you doubt anyone in the car could either. That is, if you want to help Victor."

"Sure, I do." Joe blinked several times before saying, "Only, I'm kind of broke." The frog picked at his dress and frowned. "The dress is from my neighbor. She gave it to me. And the hat."

"I'll see what I can do. Perhaps after the election we

can get you a nice cushy job."

"If you don't mind, I'd like to get something sooner than that."

From the hotel, I headed directly over to City Hall and the District Attorney's office. The young deer at the desk I talked to left the outer office and was soon back. "Sorry, but Mr. Nadel isn't in."

"When will the mouse be back?"

"He didn't say."

"Fine, I'll wait in his office." When the deer tried to stop me, I gave him a toothy grin and asked, "How much do you like your job?" After a bit of ear twitching, he shuffled back to his desk, and I walked into the District Attorney's office.

Robert Nadel looked up from whatever he was reading. "Oh, it's you. When he said, Mr. Averi wanted to see me, I thought it was someone else. That—"

"Don't worry about it. I'm here now."

The mouse was lying through his teeth, but it wasn't worth calling him out on the floor about it. We shook hands, sat down, and Nadel asked, "What can I do for you?"

"Tell me what's new."

"Nothing really. Just the same old same old." Nadel smiled like a poker player who thinks he's got a good hand, not knowing his opponent is holding a royal flush.

"And the Electioneering?"

The mouse squirmed a bit before answering. "It could be better, but everything will turn out all right."

"Anything I or Victor can help you with?" When he shook his head, I asked, "Is the talk of Victor having something to do with Ben Vale's death the worst thing you got to deal with?"

A shot of fear raced across the mouse's face, causing his whiskers to twitch, but the District Attorney recovered quickly. "Well, you understand that everyone thinks we should have cleared that case by now. People just don't understand how long things can take. Murderers don't just walk into a police station and turn themselves in."

"So, no progress? Not even a little?"

Nadel shook his head, but he was certainly wary now.

"Maybe taking it slow is a good thing. Would hate to have someone rush everything and then have the rug pulled out from under them. How's the Gordon Colbert angle going? That newt giving you any trouble?"

The mouse's mouth dropped open, and it took a full minute for him to close it before talking. "We're not sure of anything yet. Confirming his story, well you know how that goes. I didn't want to bother you with that until we were sure about everything."

"How nice that you're looking out for Victor's interests. Soon you'll be roaring like a lion. If you want to speak to the male who was with Gordon, he or rather she is at the Laurel Hotel room number four-twenty. You can't miss the frog."

Nadel didn't say anything, but he certainly looked like he was going to lose his lunch any minute.

"Victor's always willing to give the dogs in blue a hand. Do you think letting himself get arrested for murder would help?"

"I wouldn't dream of telling Victor what to do."

"Now there's a thought." The smile I gave him wasn't a nice one.

CHAPTER 8

Lenox's official company was Northside Construction and Contracting. I'd been there enough that when I walked through the door, people said hello, but didn't stop me when I headed for the door marked, private.

Inside, Lenox studied a bunch of maps and papers as a beaver fussed about pointing things out and answering questions. At my entrance, the pit bull told the beaver to collect the papers, and they'd talk later.

I made myself comfortable in a chair and asked, "How's life treating you?"

"Fine, but I might have you go out and talk to Hughes. Don't understand what's wrong with him, but he's gone shifty on us, which means we can't count on his votes. We can get along without him, but I'd like it better if he'd stayed on board."

"So the bird's jumped ship, too?"

"What do you mean?"

"Just what I said. Everyone's bailing, Victor. You've become a bad investment, and you'll remain so unless Ben Vale's murder is cleared up. It won't matter who wins the election because you'll be arrested for it, no matter what. Everyone in town thinks you killed the dog."

"Nonsense. No one wants Reg Calum running the city."

"Then why is Hughes backing down? People are suspicious because they think the police have been told not to investigate. Well, they are now. Looks like Nadel has grown a pair. I just came from his office and guess what? A couple of our guys saw you arguing with Ben that night. One headed straight to the District Attorney the other asked for money to keep quiet."

Lenox twitched and his jaw set in a scowl. "Are you sure?"

"Very. I stalled Joe Piper, but Gordon Colbert already shot his mouth off to Nadel."

"I don't mean that, I mean…" Lenox's words drifted off.

I leaned forward and stared straight at the dog. "Calum now has all the riffraff behind him, while you're counting on the respectable people for help. And they'll have no problem turning their backs on you. If fact, it will make them heroes in the public's eyes if they turn on you and toss you in jail, one of their own party members. Don't count on their loyalty, Victor, they'll lose you as soon as possible."

When the dog didn't say anything, I reiterated, "Ben Vale's murder has to be solved or you'll lose everything. Get that through your head, Victor. The sooner, the better."

"Isn't there another way?"

"No. Calum and Nadel are already nipping at your heels. Everyone else his just waiting for you to stumble."

"No, it can't happen."

I couldn't believe what I was hearing, and I tasted the air to see if there was something Lenox was smoking, but there was nothing. The dog was worried but there was no physical evidence of drugs that I could see, taste, or smell.

The bottom fell out of my stomach when he said, "I did it. I killed Ben Vale. It was an accident. The pup came at me swinging a walking stick. I must have hit him with it when I took it away from him. That's not what killed him though, the strike wasn't hard enough, but he did fall. That's when it happened. That's when the dog's head hit the curb. It was self-defense."

"Why wait this long then to say anything? Running off fouled up that option to get you off a murder charge."

"I panicked."

Warning bells sounded in my head. When the logical side of my brain ran the numbers, they didn't add up no matter how hard I tried. "Tell me everything, Victor. All the details."

Lenox's ears flattened to his head but not for long. "When I left the Vale house after dinner, Ben ran after me with a cane he'd grabbed as he ran out. We... There was some trouble, and he was upset. We both were. When he caught up with me, everything happened so fast. He swung the cane at me, and I took it away. The next thing I knew he was down on the ground with his head busted."

"Where's the cane now?"

"Gone. I burned it. When I left the scene, I didn't realize I still had it in my hand, so I tucked it under my overcoat until I could get rid of it."

"What kind of cane was it?"

The dog shrugged. "Heavy wood, rough and brown. No teeth marks."

"And his hat? Did Ben have a hat on when he confronted you? It wasn't there when I found him."

"Someone could have picked it up and walked off." Victor blinked and said, "Ben was wearing one when he caught up to me, of that I'm certain."

"Do you remember Gordon Colbert's car driving past?"

"No, but it's not like I was looking for it. The newt could have driven past at any time."

The cigar I was smoking tasted as sour as what Lenox was telling me. "Why, when you had a clear self-defense plea did you muck everything up by walking off and destroying the cane?"

"What could I do, Horace? If Wendy found out that I killed her brother, she'd never forgive me. She'd never marry me."

"Will you wake up? That female wouldn't marry you if you were the last dog on Earth. The female hates you, Victor. She believes you killed her brother, and when the police wouldn't move on the case, she started sending anonymous letters. That dalmatian turned your own pup against you. Wendy Vale came to see me this morning and tried to convince me that you were a murderer and—"

Lenox got in my face and barked, "That's enough. Do you want her for yourself, Horace? Is that it? A warm body to curl up to?"

"Listen—"

"Get out. We're done. Through. Get out."

When I got home, I broke out the Bourbon whisky and sat down with a glass to think. The telephone rang, but I didn't answer it. Not until the sun slipped down toward the horizon did I move from the chair, and pick up the receiver and call Wendy Vale. One of the servants answered on her end, and they had to go fetch her.

"Hello," she said with a voice full of curiosity, hope, and concern.

"You were right. I talked to Victor earlier today, and he didn't take well to the news of your opinion of him."

"Was it a very big argument?"

"Yes, the dog threw me out."

"I'm sorry."

"Don't be, these things happen, and we were already on thin ice."

"Will… will you be free tonight? Would you mind me coming over?"

"I'll be here. Come over anytime." We hung up, and I lay down on one of the warming rocks before the fire. I didn't intend to dose off, but I did. When I woke up, I turned on several of the lights, checked the clock, and checked in the bathroom mirror to make sure I looked presentable.

When Wendy arrived, her tail kept wagging in excitement, but she kept apologizing for the break between me and Lenox.

"Stop worrying about it. With everything that's been

going on, it would have happened sooner or later."

"I can't help feeling responsible," she said. "But I can't say I'm not glad. Did he really confess to killing Ben?"

"Yes, but apparently it was self-defense."

"Of course, he'd say that. It was murder, plain and simple." The dog bared her teeth. "Even if he's telling the truth, why can't he go through a trial just like everyone else?"

"Victor's waited too long. No one will believe him, no matter what the truth is, and he'll go straight to the electric chair."

"Then why on earth did he keep quiet?"

"You. Victor's in love with you and was afraid if you found out what he'd done, he'd lose his chance with you." I held my hands up when she looked ready to bite me. "Victor didn't know that he never had a chance. We both know your father was doing a swell job of dangling you in front of his nose, and the poor dog couldn't see anything but your spots."

"That male killed my brother. I know it, you know it, and soon everyone else will know it. Will you help me prove it?"

"No, because I believe his story. And while I understand our friendship is no more, there's no reason for me to kick him while he's down. Everyone's going to crucify him soon, with or without our help. Why not let it alone?"

"Because I have no intention of letting him alone until he's punished." The fire in the dog's eyes burned brightly. "Are you afraid to find proof that he lied to you?"

"How so?"

"Will you help me find the truth, no matter which way it leads? Proof that he is or is not lying?"

I studied her for a moment. The dog had determination. "On one condition," I said. "That whatever we find, no matter what way it points, we'll stick to it until the end. That we not only find proof, but the truth of what happened the night your brother was killed, and we don't stop until with find it all."

"Yes, of course."

"Then it's a bargain." I stuck out my hand, and we shook on it.

Before the tears that brimmed her eyes spilt out, I motioned her to a chair, and we both sat. "Let's get everything on the table, and our stories straight so that we don't tip our hand. Have you heard from Victor today?"

"No."

"Okay, that means we have no idea if Victor truly believed me or not, or if I gave him a reason to doubt his chances with you. Like I said, our friendship is over, but he's not sure where you stand, and it'll be better if we let him stew about you. Don't call him. Let him come to you. If he has doubts, calling him might cement a decision. How sure are you about him, relationship wise I mean?"

"As sure as any female can be. That sounds conceded, but I'm not sure how to explain it any other way."

"No matter, we should find out by tomorrow. Have you ever tried pumping Victor for information?"

"No."

"Did you think about hiring a private detective?"

"Yes, but how could I do that and be certain who I hired wasn't already in Victor's pocket? That's why I came to you."

I had to smile at that, and said, "I know of one we can use. But first, there's two things we need to figure out. Ben's hats, are any of them missing? Other than the one I borrowed, if we can find the missing hat, we might be able to find a clue."

"Oh dear, they're all gone. All of his things were packed up and disposed of, but even if they weren't, I don't think anyone knew how many hats he had."

"Nuts. How about his walking stick? For that matter, are any of your father's missing? A rough heavy wooden one?"

"Ben carried a silver tipped cane. It was the only one he had. The one you described would be my father's, he has several. I believe that one was a gift from someone overseas."

Excitement had me wanting to smile, but old habits kept me from reacting. "Does he still have it?"

"Yes, I think so."

"Double check and let me know."

"What is it about the stick?" Her tail thudded against the leg of the chair.

"Not sure, but Victor said Ben attacked him with a cane and described that particular one. He said he destroyed it."

"Then he's lying, I'm quite sure that stick is still in the house."

"Well somebody's certainly lying." I lean forward and put my hand on hers. "The truth. You promised. No tricks."

"No tricks."

After she left, I paced the floor. At nine-thirty, I left to talk to Joe-Josephine Piper, but when I arrived at his hotel, they told me the reed frog wasn't in.

Giving up but not wanting to deal with the silence of my own home, I headed for a place outside the city limits that served alcohol with their entertainment. The square white building wasn't much to look at, but from the amount of cars parked in front, the joint was hopping. I nodded to the doorman and walked inside. Skirting the dining room along with the orchestra, I headed for the bar in the corner of the room.

"Haven't seen you around for a while," said the moose acting as barman. "How you been?"

"Would you believe I've been behaving?"

"No, but that's okay. Manhattan?"

"Yes, please."

The bartender mixed my drink and the orchestra ended

their number just in time for a female's tipsy voice to ring shrilly through the room. "Avraham, you bastard."

I turned around to find Daniel Pearce's lady-friend at one of the tables. Daniel wasn't anywhere around, but if the red squirrel's younger companion was anything to go by, the female was trying to rope in a new sugar daddy.

With the young boar temporarily forgotten, the female glared at me. "What are you doing here? You no good louse?"

Everyone in the room was silent and looking at her. Even the bartender stopped moving the shaker he held.

"Hello, Red, have you seen Pearce since they let him out?"

"Don't you Red me." She turned to her confused companion. "And why haven't you thrown him out?"

The boar squared his shoulders, tried looking bigger than he actually was, and walked toward me. He didn't make it very far before the bull acting as bouncer picked him up and walked him out of the place.

"Looks like you lost your date, Red." I sat down at a small table and motioned her to join me. With a pout, she flounced over and dropped into a chair.

"I hate males, they're all worthless."

"Maybe you just keep picking the bad ones. Did Pearce skip on you?"

"Yeah, the scum."

A skunk brought my Manhattan over along with a drink for the red squirrel. He gave me a questioning glance, and I nodded that it was all right.

"Have you eaten anything, Red? Would you like anything?"

"This is fine," she said, sipping at her drink.

I turned to the skunk. "I'll have steak with a side of eggs and whatever vegetable you have that doesn't come out of a can."

When the waiter left, the red squirrel sulked over her drink and shed a few tears. "You played a lousy trick on me."

"Not me. Pearce did that. He didn't have to haul off with my money then take your jewels to pay up."

When the orchestra started back up, she said, "Let's dance," and I followed her out to the dance floor. "I'm on one hell of a streak this year. Pearce, Vale, and now you."

"Ben Vale?"

"Who else? Though I have to admit I was still with Pearce and didn't go over to his place very often."

"So you were one of the females that met him at the apartment he rented?"

"Yeah, what of it?" She looked at me warily.

"Let me buy you another drink."

The doorbell woke me a few minutes after nine in the morning, and I crawled out of bed to answer it. Wendy Vale was on the other side and looked slightly embarrassed seeing me in my robe and slippers.

"Sorry, I didn't mean to wake you, but I just had to talk to you. I tried calling last night, but you were out." I stepped back to allow her inside and got thumped by her wagging tail as she passed. "All father's walking sticks are accounted for. I checked them several times and they're all there. Victor Lenox is a liar."

"The heavy brown one?"

"Right where it's supposed to be in the holder of the foyer."

"Then he did lie." I rubbed my face attempting to wipe the sleep from my eyes.

"There's more." Wendy's tail stopped wagging and her ears drooped. "Victor showed up yesterday at the house. He was there when I got home." The dog shivered before continuing. "He asked me to marry him."

"What did you say?"

"As much as I wanted to tell him to go to hell, I held my tongue and told him that it was still to soon after Ben's death to consider big decisions like that. I didn't say no, but I think we have an understanding. An unofficial engagement you might say."

The female looked away. "Don't look at me like that. It's not like I'm trying to be heartless. I just thought it would be better if I was in a position where he talked to me. That's what we wanted, isn't it?"

"True. I just can't help thinking what kind of fix he'd be in if you loved him as much as you hated him."

She gave me a glare that could curdle milk for that comment. "Not funny."

"Have you eaten?"

"No, I was too excited."

"What would you like? I'll order breakfast and have it sent up. Make yourself comfortable while I get dressed."

Wendy agreed and took her coat off while I slipped into my dressing room. When I returned, the telephone rang and without thinking I picked it up. "Hello?"

"Hello, Horace? This is Joe, I mean Josephine. I got a message that you were trying to get hold of me."

"Yes, I wanted to ask you about the male you'd seen Victor with. Did he have a hat on?"

"Sure he did. Nobody goes out without a hat. That would stick out like a sore thumb."

"What about a walking stick, did he have one of those?"

"Not that I saw. Hey, Horace, did you talk to Victor about… Um… my situation?"

"Not really, I didn't get the chance to go over the details. Why don't you go talk to him yourself?"

"You sure it'll be okay?"

"Yeah, no problem." We said our goodbyes, and I returned the receiver to its cradle. Wendy's eyes watched me curiously. "That was one of the people who saw Victor and your brother arguing that night. There was no stick, but Ben was wearing a hat. Granted it was dark, and neither person is nocturnal, so I doubt they saw much."

"Why are you so interested in the hat? Is it really that

important?"

"I'm just an amateur detective grasping at straws, but I will say that the hat keeps bugging me. It's been bugging me since I found your brother's body."

"Have you learned anything else since yesterday?" she asked.

"Not really. I met up with one of the females Ben played around with, but she didn't have anything to add. Dead end."

"Do I know her?"

"No, and before you ask, it wasn't Amy. She still thinks her father killed Ben because of her, and the only reason she thinks that is because of your letters and the newspaper. Amy's too naïve, too trusting, and too much of a romantic to realize his death had nothing to do with her."

Wendy nodded, but I could tell she wasn't completely convinced. Breakfast came, and we ate in relative silence before the telephone rang again. This time when I answered it, the caller was Victor Lenox's mother. "Hello, Mom, how are you?"

"Oh, Horace, I'm so glad I reached you. I have no idea what to do, and I can't get hold of Victor."

"Slow down and breathe. Tell me what happened."

"An officer from the District Attorney's office is here and wants to speak to Amy. What do I do?"

"Let them. I don't think you can stop them, and I doubt if it will do any harm."

"If you're sure. Is Victor with you?"

"Sorry, Mom, he's not here, and I don't know where he is."

"I do wish he was here to deal with this. It's so… it's so disconcerting."

"I know it is, but it will be all right. Stay with Amy while they question her, she's still underage. And like I said, I doubt if she knows anything."

After reassuring the old dog, I hung up the telephone

and looked at Wendy. "Seems you weren't the only one thinking Amy might know something. Nadel sent someone to question her. That was Victor's mother."

"Why did she call you?"

"Because she can't get hold of Victor and hoped I knew where he was. Apparently, Victor hasn't told her about the argument we had." I studied the dalmatian for a moment before saying, "I had a dream about you. Not a particularly nice one, but it does make me question your determination to follow this through."

"I want Ben's killer brought to justice, no matter what the cost." Wendy cocked her head to the side and asked, "What happened in the dream? Surely someone like you doesn't believe in dreams."

"I'm a gambler first and foremost. While I don't believe in anything, I do look at everything. It helps figure out the odds. As for the dream. I was fishing and caught the biggest fish ever. You said you wanted to look at it, but you tossed it back into the water before I could do anything."

She laughed and asked, "Then what did you do?"

"Other than wake up, nothing I could do."

"Well I promise not to throw any fish you ever catch back in the water." The dog smiled. "I had a dream about you, too. Only we were lost in the woods and starving. We came across a house that when we looked through the window, we could see a banquet set, but no one would answer the door. Then we found a screw under the doormat that fit the lock. Only when we opened the door, the room's floor was covered in carnivorous beetles, and we shut and locked the door. You had the idea of climbing on the roof and letting the beetles out so we could get to the food after they all left, and it worked."

"That sounds more like a fanciful story than a dream."

"It's true."

"Some perhaps, but not all of it."

"Has anyone ever told you that you're a brute?" she

asked.

"A few." I picked up my fork but didn't eat. "Does your father know what you're up to? Does he know anything, or have you even questioned him?"

"I know he knows something."

"The problem is, he might go off on you, right? The old dog has a temper, doesn't he?"

She looked away, and I figured I had my answer before she said a word. "Yes, it's true he... I'm sure we can make him understand how important everything is, he'll understand. Can we tell him now?"

"No, not yet. Hopefully we can see him tomorrow. There are still a few other things I need to check out."

"You'll let me know as soon as possible, won't you?"

"Yes, but I hope you'll be able to deal with the consequences."

CHAPTER 9

After Wendy Vale left, I called David and asked the rabbit to drop by. He agreed, and we were soon enjoying a glass of Bourbon whisky and mineral water in front of the fire.

"Did you hear about Victor and I splitting?" I asked.

"For the second time? Yes, but I figure it's another ruse, to mess with Reg Calum, so does everyone else."

"Really? Well, I can tell you that this time it's for real. Victor and I are no longer friends."

"Shame."

When David didn't say anything further, I asked, "What do I owe you?"

"Thirty dollars and we're square."

I pulled a roll of bills from my pocket, peeled off three tens, and handed them to him.

"Much obliged," said David, and stuck the bills in his pocket.

"If you're interested, I'd like to know more about Victor's involvement in Ben Vale's murder. Let's just say I wouldn't mind finding the dirt on him."

"Sorry, no can do. My business is doing good, and I don't want to mess it up. Whichever side wins the election makes no difference to me, but messing with Victor can get me run out of town at best. The thought of someone using my feet as their lucky charm doesn't sit well with me."

"Victor's crew is ready to toss him over."

"And they might, or they might not. Victor's a fighter, and we both understand that even if they arrest him, getting the charges to stick will be difficult. No thanks. I'd rather not tempt fate."

I nodded. "That's fine. If you won't, you won't. No hard feelings. Just one more question. Do you have any idea where I could find Reg Calum?"

David's whiskers moved, and his ears did that funny thing rabbits do when they're thinking. "The third time the police raided his place, a couple of coppers got killed, so the weasel is keeping out of sight. The cops don't have anything on him personally, but he's not taking any chances. Do you know Pat Bloom?" When I nodded, David said, "If you talk to that iguana, he might be able to tell you. He usually hangs out at Russell's place on Fifth."

"Thanks, David."

"Anytime." The rabbit opened his mouth but didn't say anything more. Instead, he closed it and nodded.

This time when I arrived at the District Attorney's office, I wasn't stonewalled but ushered right into Robert Nadel's office.

The mouse stayed seated behind his desk and remained cold but polite. "How do you do, Avraham?"

I sat down and lit a cigar. "Thought you might want to know what happened the last time I talked to Victor. About how you seemed jumpy and was trying to hang a murder charge on him. He believed me but didn't like my advice about solving the pup's murder. That's when the dog confessed to me that he killed Ben Vale. Self-defense of course."

The mouse didn't say a word, but the way his left eye and whiskers twitched, the news didn't set well with him.

"No trick, honest. You're a timid soul, Nadel, but believe me when I say I'm willing to sign a statement as to what was said. Would you like me to do so? I'd hate to waste your time if you'd rather not."

Nadel pressed a button on his desk, and a secretary came in. The giraffe looked at the mouse expectantly. "Yes, sir?"

"Mr. Avraham wants to make a statement, if you

wouldn't mind taking it down and have it typed up so he can sign it, please."

"Yes, sir."

The giraffe sat down in a chair, and I recited what happened in Victor's office with as much detail as I could. When I was finished, the giraffe left Nadel's office, and we waited in silence until she returned with the typed up version.

Once signed, I handed the paper to Nadel. "I thought you'd be pleased. Maybe even haul Victor in an have him explain everything."

"If you don't mind, I'd rather run my own office."

"Of course, but I must admit, this isn't as fun as I'd expected. See you later, Nadel, and be careful when crossing streets."

That night I drove to Russell's house over on Fifth. The three-story house was dark with blackout shades, but when I rang the doorbell, the otter that opened the door nodded and let me in. Twenty feet down a darkened hallway, I opened a door on the left and walked down a flight of steps into the basement. The armadillo playing bartender was tuning the radio to one of the music stations.

At the other end of the bar, a door marked Privy opened, and an alligator stepped through. Tom took one look at me and smiled showing several of his missing teeth. "Well look who's here. You come back for another pummeling, Avraham?"

"Hello, Tom."

The patrons glanced at us, and one or two decided to leave, but most looked on in morbid fascination.

The alligator swaggered over and not only grabbed my hand but put an arm around my shoulders and pulled me over to the bar. "This is the best guy I ever bruised a knuckle on. Swell, real swell. How about a drink?"

I didn't struggle but nodded to the bartender. "Scotch."

Tom's ruckus laughter had everyone cringing. "You're a real... what is it they call it? Masochist. You're a real masochist, you are."

Only when the bartender set our drinks down in front of us did Tom let me go. From the way he was acting, he was well on his way to becoming pickled.

I barely got my drink down before he got hold of me again. "Why don't we go upstairs? I've got a room that's small enough for me to pound on you and not have to pick you up off the floor every time."

"How about another drink?"

"Why not?"

Another drink down, and the big male steered me toward the stairs. Only we didn't stop at the first floor, but on the second. The room he pushed me into had a couch, several chairs, and two tables. A couple of empty glasses and a plate with the remains of a sandwich sat on one table.

Tom made a noise similar to a motorboat before bellowing, "Now, where is she? Do you see a broad in here?"

"Sorry, nobody here but us chickens." I had no idea what he was talking about.

"Huh?" The alligator stared at me for a minute before shoving me onto the couch. "Have a seat." Tom turned, not paying attention to where his tail landed and knocked over several chairs on his way back to the door to press a bell button set into the jamb.

The drunken alligator rambled on about the missing female and broken chairs before an otter poked his head through the door. "What can I get you?"

"Where've you been? Me and my friend could've died from thirst."

The waiter glanced at me, but stayed calm as Tom ranted, ending in, "Where's the broad?"

"She left the building."

That set Tom off on another tangent before the waiter

could escape to get our drinks. When he came back, Tom downed his and sent the otter back for another.

"I know what you're up to, Avraham." The alligator's breath could asphyxiate a person at twenty paces, and I kept my tongue in my mouth.

"Really? You knew I was looking for Pat Bloom, hoping he'd direct me to where I could find Reg Calum."

"Don't you think I know where Calum is?" The alligator roared his displeasure.

An armadillo poked his head through the door and said, "Keep it down, Tom. You're making enough noise to wake the dead."

"He thinks I don't know what he's up to, Russell. What do you think of that?"

"None of my business, but since your shouting it out, I guess you're making it everyone's business." Russell gave me a wink and ducked back out the door.

Tom would have gone on another rant had the waiter not brought another round, but it only quieted the drunken male long enough to down the glass. That's when he started calling me every name in the book before stating, "You're trying to get me drunk so you can tie me up and hand me over to the cops, aren't you?"

"Well, you are wanted for shooting Jason East."

"To hell with that deer. Did you know him?"

I shook my head. "Why don't I buy you another drink?"

"Yeah, why not?" Tom poked his thick finger at the button and swore a blue streak before the otter showed up again after which the male announced, "Do you really think they'd fry me?"

"With potatoes and grilled onions."

The comment flew over Tom's head and he pounded the table as he bellowed, "I got a lot on Calum."

The weasel in question slipped through the door, frowning with displeasure. "Go ahead, Tom, why don't you tell everyone?"

Tom squinted at the weasel and grinned. "Hey, Reg, come on in and have a drink."

"I think you've had enough. Didn't I tell you to keep a low profile?"

"This is a speakeasy; how much lower can I go?"

Calum ignored the alligator and asked, "How much did you get out of him?"

"Nothing that made any sense," I said.

"I told you before, Tom, that you talked too much. Maybe you'd still have all your teeth if you closed your mouth once in a while."

The pair bickered like a couple of old timers before the weasel tried shoving the alligator back into his seat. Tom swung at Calum with one of his meaty fists and missed. The weasel reached for something at his back, and I joined the fray, grabbing Calum's arm before he could reach the pistol. I disarmed the weasel while Tom grabbed the male by the neck.

"So you was going to shoot me? I don't like that."

Gun in hand, I backed away from the pair and watched in horror as Tom squeezed the life out of Calum. The alligator was truly insane. The male tossed the limp body on the vacated couch and grinned. "Let's get out of here before anyone gets wind of what we done. Give me the gun."

"I don't think so, Tom." I pointed the gun at him. This wasn't what I had planned. "We can say it was self-defense, and as long as we keep to the same story we'll get away with it."

"That's a nice idea. Only they want me for East. Damn deer. I should have shot them all."

"Keep back, Tom. I'll have no trouble shooting you. Remember, I still owe you one."

"You're a heel."

"Sit down, Tom."

While he dropped into a chair, I sidled over to the bell and pressed it.

"Do you really think they'll drag me out of here, Avraham? This is my hang out."

"Not anymore, Tom. Without Calum, you're nothing, and nobody wants you around. Keep your hands where I can see them."

When the waiter popped his head in, I said, "Get Russell and fast. We have a problem."

The otter disappeared, and the armadillo returned. Russell took one look at the gun in my hand, and the body on the couch and said, "Jesus, Mary, and Joseph. What the hell happened up here?"

"Tom killed Calum. Get the place cleaned up and call the police. Also, call a doctor just in case Calum's not dead."

"He's dead. I don't strangle someone and not do it right. Now tell this idiot to hand over the gun and that he's not getting away with this."

Russell glanced at Tom then at me but didn't say a word.

"Get the place cleaned up. You'll be fine as long as you do that before the police show up. Get going."

Tom started bellowing again, and Russell ducked out of the room. It didn't take long for the police to show up and take the alligator off my hands. I handed the gun over to one of the officers and watched as two mastiffs and a hippo put the handcuffs on Tom and hauled him out of the room.

When the officer in charge asked me what happened, I told him everything, leaving nothing out. The doctor that came in pronounced Calum dead and let the buzzards bring in a basket to take the body away.

I didn't get out of police headquarters until after midnight, having answered all their questions and signed my statement. The taxi out front of the station expelled a pair of journalists, and I crawled inside giving Lenox's address.

When I got there, Mrs. Lenox opened the door. "Oh,

Horace, I thought you were Victor."

"He isn't here?"

"No, and I don't have a clue where he's gone off to now."

The old dog was stressed, and her tail was tucked between her legs.

"What's the matter, Mom?"

"It's Amy. She… she tried to commit suicide. The doctor has her sedated and bandaged, but says she'll be fine unless she tries again."

"What happened?"

"She tried cutting her wrists. There was so much blood."

I held her in my arms as the old dog cried on my shoulder. After a while she asked, "Is it true, have you broken with Victor?"

"I'm afraid so."

"Can it be fixed?"

"No, not this time, Mom."

"It's because of that Wendy female, isn't it?"

"Would you tell Victor that I came by to see him, and that I'll be waiting at home for him to stop by?"

CHAPTER 10

Back home I drank coffee and did everything I could to fill the time until daybreak. After breakfast around nine in the morning, I called Wendy Vale. When she came on the line, she sounded excited and said, "Hello."

"Hello, yourself. Are you ready for the fireworks?"

"We're telling him today?"

"Sure thing. Is your father there? Let's tell him together," I said.

"Yes, we're just about to sit down and have breakfast."

"Great, I'll leave right now. Promise not to say a word until I get there."

"I promise."

We hung up, and I headed to the closet and bundled for the weather. It was hard not to fidget on the drive over, but I managed it. When the maid came to the door, I said, "Wendy Vale is expecting me."

The grouse nodded and led me into the dining room where the Senator and his daughter sat eating. Wendy bounded from her chair, tail wagging, to greet me. "You're here, wonderful."

The Senator frowned briefly at his daughter's exuberance but remained cordial. "Good morning, Mr. Avraham. Please join us."

"No thanks, I've already eaten. I'm actually here with some news. Atop some strong evidence, Victor Lenox confessed to the murder of your son."

The dalmatian's eyes narrowed but otherwise showed no reaction. "What evidence?"

"His confession is the biggest piece. He said Ben ran after him with a walking stick, and in disarming him, he accidently killed him. As for the stick, he said he burned it, but your daughter said it was here. So Victor lied about the stick."

"It is, I checked, it's in the stand with all the others." Wendy's tail was going a mile a minute, and the rest of her couldn't keep still.

"That tanks Victor's story," I said. "At least the self-defense part. I told Nadel yesterday and signed an affidavit to the fact. He'll have to pick up the pit bull today, there's no other choice."

Wendy stopped bouncing. She cocked her head to the side but didn't say a word.

"Is there anything else?" asked the Senator.

"That's the main thing. Isn't that enough?"

The dalmatian rose from his chair. "If you'll excuse me for a moment. Do please stay. I just need a moment to myself, if you please."

When the dog left the room, I leaned down to whisper to Wendy. "Is he likely to do something rash? Like go after Victor?"

"I don't know."

"Is there someplace we can keep watch and prevent him from leaving the house?"

"The front parlor."

"Let's go."

We moved from the dining room to the front parlor and waited. Wendy tried asking another question, but I shushed her to silence.

The Senator wasn't too long in arriving, wearing his coat and hat, heading for the front door. I stepped out to block him. "I wouldn't do that, Senator Vale. It'll only cause more trouble."

"Do listen to him, father."

"I'm in a hurry. Now, would you please let me pass?"

"Not with that gun you have in your pocket."

Wendy let out a whine as the Senator bared his teeth briefly. "Wendy, go to your room."

She almost did, but after the first step, she turned back and said, "No."

I placed my hand on the Senator's arm and motioned to the parlor. "Perhaps we should discuss this." With my other hand, I pulled out my official documents. "I'm still appointed as a special investigator to the District Attorney's office, and I'd rather not have to arrest you, sir."

"Are you trying to save your murdering friend?"

"I think you know better."

The stare down the dog gave me wasn't bad for a mammal, but he finally said, "If you don't mind my dear, please leave us for a moment so that Mr. Avraham and I can talk in private."

She looked at me in question before walking back down the hall with ears flattened and tail down.

"How long?" asked the Senator.

"I've only been investigating for two days. Your daughter's been doing it from the start. She hates Victor and has always believed he murdered Ben."

"What?"

The surprise on the dog's face was genuine. He hadn't known his daughter's feelings, and probably never bothered to ask.

"Yes, she'd probably flip the switch to Old Sparky herself if they'd let her."

The Senator stepped into the parlor, and I followed, closing the door. "I'm not a bloodthirsty dog, but I'll be dammed if I'm going to let my son's murderer go free."

"I told you, Nadel will be picking Victor up. And don't worry about them not doing it. They're all ready to turn on him. A bit of courage and everyone will be pounding at his door."

"You know as well as I do, that will never happen. Even with a temporary rebellion, Victor still runs the city."

"Not anymore. Now, if you would please, hand over the gun." I put my hand out, but the dog wouldn't budge.

I had to force it from him and in the process a chair was knocked over. The ruckus brought Wendy into the room, and she arrived in time to see me drop the gun in my own pocket.

"What happened?" she asked.

"Nothing much, but I had to take his gun away from him."

"Get out of my house," growled the Senator.

"Not this time. It's time the truth comes out. You killed your son, Senator. Ben ran after Victor that night, and while I'm not sure if either you or he grabbed the walking stick, you're the one who struck him down. The only reason you want to leave this house is that you can't risk Victor being arrested and telling everyone what really happened. You'll be able to get off a murder charge with the avenging father routine."

The Senator didn't move a muscle, nor did he deny anything I said. Wendy on the other hand, whined and sunk to the floor in horror.

"Had Victor known Wendy hated him and thought he killed Ben; he'd have never gone with the plan. What really happened, Senator? Did you see your chances of getting re-elected go down the drain because your son refused to do what he was told? You couldn't have that could you?"

"This is nonsense."

"Is it really? You mean you didn't take the murder weapon back home. That and Ben's hat, seeing as you left the house without your own."

"Victor confessed," he growled.

"Why don't we call Victor and have him come over to explain himself. Things might get interesting when he finds out you planned to shoot him. Wendy, do you mind telephoning Victor?"

"This is ridiculous."

"Is it?"

Wendy stood on stiff legs and headed to the telephone.

"Wait," barked the Senator. "Mr. Avraham, can we

speak alone?"

Before I could answer, Wendy barked back, "No, you're not shutting me out this time. I want to know."

"Wendy—"

"Tell me."

The dog pulled a handkerchief out and wiped his face before speaking. "I didn't want to lose Victor's friendship because of my son, so yes, I did follow them. Ben was barking his head off while Victor just stood and stared at him. I told Victor to leave, that I'd handle Ben, but Ben... The things he said, no father should hear. The next thing I knew, he was on the ground. Victor gave me Ben's hat and told me to go home, that we couldn't afford the scandal, that he would take care of everything. Like a fool, I did what I was told."

"Nice speech," I said. "A bit too theatrical, but then again, you are a professional politician. Just enough truth to make it sound believable."

"You left him there?" said Wendy, her voice hurt and hollow. "In the street?"

The Senator didn't say anything at first, but his ears flattened briefly. "Mr. Avraham, would you mind leaving me alone for five minutes with my pistol?"

"Not a chance. You're not taking the cowards way out."

I walked Nadel to the front door of the Vale house. The Senator had already been handcuffed and taken away.

"Are you coming with us?" asked the mouse.

"No, I'm done for now."

Nadel grinned from ear to ear. "Well, stop by anytime. You might trick me, but if your tricks result in things like this, I'll welcome them."

"Sure thing."

He walked out smiling, and I closed the door behind him. Wendy had stayed in the sitting room, and I met her there. "They're all gone now. Your father made a statement with a little more detail than what he gave us, but I'm not sure how much of it was true."

"Will they send him to the electric chair?"

"Doubt it. Between his age and prominence, I'd say manslaughter with a suspended sentence."

"Do you think my father killed Ben by accident?"

"Not a chance."

With ears flattened, she let out another whine. "Was he really going to shoot Victor?"

"To save his own hide, yes."

"I hated Victor, I still do even though I realize he's innocent, but you… I liked you, and I still do. Why?"

There was no answer for that, so I just shrugged.

"How long did you know the truth? About my father?"

"Not sure. I'll admit I never liked him, and Victor understood this. That's probably why the silly pit bull gave me that story of killing Ben so that I wouldn't tank his chances with you."

"And you don't like me."

"You're all right, and you've paid dearly for what you've done in your own right. That's enough."

"You and Victor can be friends again," she said.

"No, not this time. This time, I'm leaving town on the four-thirty train."

"Take me with you."

The pronouncement took me aback. "A bit hysterical, are we?"

"Maybe, but I need to get away from here. Please? I don't think I could leave here on my own. I've never…" Her words drifted off.

"You've never been out in the real world."

Wendy nodded, but her eyes stayed on the floor. Like a dope, I said, "Pack light. We can send for everything else later."

Tears brimmed in her eyes, but at least her tail wagged briefly. The dog ran out of the room and soon came back dressed in a black coat and hat, carrying two suitcases.

Wendy and I rode in silence back to my place, so I could grab my own bags. When we got there, she said, "I lied about my dream, the ending. The screw was made of crystal and broke in the lock. The beetles swarmed us, and I woke up screaming."

"A nightmare, it was just a nightmare."

"Where are we heading?"

"New York. After that, we can go anywhere you'd like." The doorbell rang, interrupting the conversation, and I motioned toward the bedroom while moving her bags.

Once she was hidden away, I opened the front door to find Victor on the other side.

"You were right, Horace, about everything. I'm sorry."

"There's nothing to be sorry about. Come on in."

Victor spotted the bags in the living room. "Are you leaving?"

"Yes." When Victor didn't say anything, I asked, "How's Amy?"

"She'll be okay. It was all my fault."

Anything I could say would have rubbed salt into his wounds, so I kept my mouth shut.

"Will you be saying goodbye to her and Mom?"

"I'll leave that to you. The train leaves at four-thirty. With Calum dead, what are you going to do with your not so faithful henchmen?"

"Calum's thugs can run the city for the next four years while I clean house. They'll make a muck of it, but I'll get it back by then."

"You could get it back now."

"No, I'm tired, and I need to clean house." There was a defeated edge to the pit bull's words. "You're not holding anything against me, are you, Horace?"

"No, but I still have to go." I stuck out my hand, and he took it in a crushing grip.

"I wish you'd stay."

"You'll do fine without me."

Victor nodded and let go.

"Wendy is here," I said. The pit bull blinked as the dalmatian walked into the room. "She asked me to be her chaperon on her travels."

Victor mumbled a few unintelligible words and left the apartment. Wendy looked at me as I stared at the door feeling empty.

COLLECT ALL THE POACHED PARODIES BOOKS

THE LIZARD FIFTH
Scarlet Crop
The Lamarre Curse
The Persian Penguin
The Crystal Screw
The Lean Male

KAISER WRENCH
I, the Tribunal
My Claws are Quick
Retribution is Mine!
A Solitary Evening
The Great Slay
Pet Me Fatal
The Female Trackers
The Worm
The Contorted Figure
The Figure Fans
Existence…Eliminated
The Carnage Male
Dark Lane

LUCIUS ANORAQ
The Long Slumber
Goodbye Gorgeous
The Lofty Perch
The Female in the Water
The Wee Sibling
The Lengthy Farewell
Recap

For more information go to www.stacybender.net

Made in the USA
Columbia, SC
14 July 2023

20281054R00067